PUSHKIN

THE S

HELME

MANOR

'An intriguing mystery tale... with a layered mystery to solve and a satisfying emotional resolution'

***Big Issue*, Kids' Books of the Year**

'Ideal to snuggle up with on a chilly evening, this evocative, gentle ghost story for 9+ has a hint of *Tom's Midnight Garden*'

Guardian

'An authentic classic ghost story that speaks to Victorian traditions, while also bringing an accessible modern sensibility... It would make an excellent advent gift'

Irish Times

'So compelling and absorbing that it is impossible to put down! A brilliant, gripping story – perfect for Christmas, but a great read at any time of year'

Through the Bookshelf

'Carefully placed clues, shiver inducing sightings and layers of questions that allow the reader to really be a part of the story... A spine-tingling Christmas mystery'

Scope for Imagination

—ALSO BY EVA FRANTZ—

The Mystery of Raspberry Hill

EVA FRANTZ is a Finnish author and journalist. She was already an award-winning writer of crime novels for grown-ups when she wrote her first book for children, *The Mystery of Raspberry Hill,* which won the Runeberg Junior Prize. She currently lives in a lovely yellow house in Esbo with a lovely husband and three mostly lovely children. *The Secret of Helmersbruk Manor* is her second spooky book for children published by Pushkin Press.

A.A. PRIME is an award-winning translator from Swedish to English. Her previous translations for Pushkin Children's include Maria Turtschaninoff's *Red Abbey Chronicles* trilogy.

ELIN SANDSTRÖM is an illustrator, artist and writer living outside of Stockholm, Sweden. She has been working as an illustrator since 2012 and in 2023 made her debut as an author with *Vilse* (*Lost*).

THE SECRET OF HELMERSBRUK MANOR

A CHRISTMAS MYSTERY

Eva Frantz

Illustrated by

Elin Sandström

Translated from the Swedish by A.A. Prime

PUSHKIN CHILDREN'S

Pushkin Press
Somerset House, Strand
London WC2R 1LA

Published by agreement with Helsinki Literary Agency

The Secret of Helmersbruk Manor was first published as *Hemligheten i Helmersbruk* by Bonnier Carlsen and Schildts & Söderströms in Helsinki, 2021

First published by Pushkin Press in 2023
This edition published 2024

This work has been published with the financial assistance of FILI – Finnish Literature Exchange

1 3 5 7 9 8 6 4 2

ISBN 13: 978-1-78269-420-5

Designed and typeset by Tetragon, London
Printed and bound in the United Kingdom by Clays Ltd, Elcograf S.p.A.

www.pushkinpress.com

THE SECRET OF
HELMERSBRUK MANOR

Long have I existed.

I remember when all the trees on the avenue were tender saplings and the ships on the horizon had masts and sails.

I have heard the terrified screams of newborns and relieved sighs of the dying.

I have seen joy and sorrow, wealth and poverty, blooming and withering.

Every year the first sunbeams of spring return and fill me with hope.

But now I can feel the last of my hope draining away.

I have waited.

Waited.

And waited.

The living have forgotten about me.

The dead think only of themselves.

Long has it been since I was somebody's pride and joy.

Surely the time will soon come when I am destroyed for ever.

But not just yet.

I have one final chance.

And I am taking it now.

THE GATEKEEPER'S COTTAGE

1ST DECEMBER 1975

They travelled to the seaside on the first of December. Flora had written it on the kitchen calendar in red biro, which looked both Christmassy and angry:

To Helmersbruk!!!

No sane person goes to the seaside in the middle of winter. The whole point of a seaside holiday is to swim in the sea, play in the sand and tan your legs. But Mum didn't care. She was utterly convinced that a month by the sea was exactly what they needed, she and Flora.

Instead of a parasol and swimming costumes, they packed their warmest jumpers, woolly tights and boots. Flora had to bring all her school books as well. Her teacher had given her a long list of tasks to complete before Christmas. Flora had already done a lot of them before they left. She found that schoolwork didn't take long when she had peace and quiet, and no one throwing breadcrumbs in her hair or calling her Filthy Flora.

Mum had packed her orange typewriter. She was going to write her next book while Flora was doing her schoolwork. In the evenings they would make a fire in the open hearth, eat sausage sandwiches and play cards, Mum said.

The whole part about the sandwiches and fireplace sounded cosy enough, but Flora wasn't convinced. Mum got big ideas sometimes, and now that Dad wasn't around any more to rein in her wild plans, Flora had no choice but to go along with them. She was pleased about missing some school, but did they really have to go so far away?

When they got off the bus Flora was even more dubious.

What sort of place was Helmersbruk anyway? Everything was dark and gloomy. When the bus drove away they couldn't see a single other person anywhere, even though they seemed to be in the middle of a small town of some sort.

'Everyone is probably at home eating dinner,' Mum speculated. 'Come on, let's go.'

'Is it far?' Flora groaned.

Her rucksack weighed a tonne and she was holding a big plastic bag full of bedsheets in one hand and a travel bag of clothes in the other.

'No, not at all,' said Mum but it was clear from her voice that she had no idea.

As soon as they started walking they became swallowed up in a close, dense fog. It was getting dark and the lights of the street lamps looked like monstrous fireflies hovering above them. Then, to make matters worse, a drizzling rain began to fall.

They walked and walked. Flora's legs grew weak and the handles of the heavy bags cut into her hands and formed creases in her palms. She had to bite her lip to stop herself from asking 'Are we there yet?' the whole time like a little kid.

The street lights coloured the road orange and everything else was black. From time to time Flora thought she could see a solitary light on the right-hand side of the road. Maybe there were houses there? But none of them were their destination.

'I need a rest,' Flora whined and dropped the bags.

The thump they made on the ground echoed slightly and Flora realized that they were standing on a bridge. There was a railing on both sides and she could hear water rushing somewhere far below. How high was this bridge?

Flora left the bags where they were and went to peer over the railing.

All she could see was darkness, no water. Could she be standing above a vast chasm?

She rushed to catch up with Mum.

'It can't be far now,' Mum said, but she wasn't convincing either of them.

After the bridge the street lights became fewer and further apart, and in the darkness between the lights they couldn't even see their own feet. But Flora could tell that they were getting close to the sea anyway, because the wind was strong and smelt salty and rotten.

Suddenly Mum came to a halt and shouted:

'Look, Passad Road! We must be close.'

The name of the road was written on a sign mounted on a very high brick wall, beyond which they saw a house. It was a very old little house, made of the same bricks as the wall, as though they were part of the same residence.

'Is this where we're going to live?' Flora said.

'I think so.'

'How do we even get in?'

'There's a gate in the wall over there. Come on, I'm freezing!'

Mum grabbed the handle of the little gate. First she pulled, then she pushed. The gate refused to open.

'Oh, what in the name of?...' Mum sighed.

'Shall I try?'

'Be my guest, but I think it must have rusted shut or something.'

Mum stepped to one side and Flora pressed the handle.

The gate swung open with a gentle squeak. It almost sounded like it said, 'Ha ha.'

Mum burst out laughing.

'How did you do that?'

'I just pulled it. It wasn't even stiff. Come on.'

They walked through the gate and around the side of the house, where they found some steps leading up to the front door.

'I guess we'd better knock?' said Mum.

'Go on then!'

Flora hadn't meant to snap, but she couldn't help it.

What had Mum got them into? It was dark and cold and horrible and this house was... well, how to describe it? Very lonely. There was something melancholy about it. Were they really going to stay here for a whole month? In a sad little house surrounded by vast, dense darkness?

But then the door opened and a warm light spilt out on to the steps. In the doorway stood a man in late middle age. He looked a little stern but not in the least unpleasant.

'Ah yes. There, you see,' he said with a thoughtful expression.

It struck Flora as a rather odd thing to say. 'Welcome' or 'How was your journey?' would have been traditional. But instead, the man waved them in and watched them curiously as they lugged their bags up the stairs.

He was short for a grown man, even shorter than Flora, who was only twelve years old. He had round cheeks, fair downy hair that stuck out in all directions, and pale blue eyes. He looked like a mix between a rather grumpy gnome and an overgrown child.

'Good afternoon!' Mum shouted embarrassingly loudly.

The house was warm and filled with the strong but pleasant smell of an open fireplace. The house looked miserable from the outside, but inside it was cosy.

Flora dropped her bags on the hallway floor and let out a sigh.

'It's raining, I see,' mumbled the man, looking at their wet cheeks. 'We can only hope it doesn't get icy and slippery.'

Mum took off her glove and held out her hand.

'Nice to meet you. I'm Linn Winter and this is Flora.'

'Good. I'm Fridolf. I live next door.'

Flora pulled off her shoes and stepped into the little living room. Two armchairs stood in front of a crackling fire. She supposed that was where they would sit and eat their sausage sandwiches. A door was open on to a kitchen with lemon-yellow cabinets and a staircase in the hallway led to an upper floor.

'Oh, this is just lovely,' said Mum.

Fridolf nodded seriously.

'Aye,' he said. 'I've always liked the Gatekeeper's Cottage.'

'Gatekeeper's Cottage?'

'Aye. Not that there's any need for a gatekeeper these days. Me, I live over in the Washhouse.'

'Why do you live in a washhouse?' asked Flora.

'It's not used for laundry any more; I've made it into a home. The Gatekeeper's Cottage is too big. The Washhouse does me just fine.'

Flora had always thought a washhouse was the sort of laundry room that blocks of flats might have in the basement. But it made more sense that a washhouse would be a building in its own right.

'Are there lots of buildings here?' she asked.

'Aye. There's the garage and the stables. A few cottages, the orangery, and then the manor house, of course.'

Flora was taken aback.

A manor house!

Mum hadn't said anything about that!

Flora had always loved old houses. She dreamt that one day she might live in a grand old mansion instead of a boring urban flat. She would probably have to win the lottery or something.

The Gatekeeper's Cottage must be old as well, but it wasn't exactly luxurious. Flora hoped the manor house would be huge and beautiful. She would have gladly run off to take a look straight away, but it was too dark out.

'Does anyone live in the manor?' she asked.

Fridolf shook his head.

'No. No one's lived in the von Hiems manor for nigh on fifty years.'

Fridolf and Mum disappeared into the kitchen. Mum was babbling on in a loud voice and Fridolf muttered something about water pipes and valves. Flora didn't think he seemed especially pleased to see them. Why rent out a house if you don't want guests? But on the other hand, Flora found it irritating when people wore big fake grins on their faces all the time. She would prefer a grumpy but kindly little old man any day.

She went up the stairs to the first floor. She found herself on a small landing with three doors, opened the nearest one and walked into a bedroom with flowery wallpaper. In the corner was an old-fashioned bed with a coiling metal headboard and small bedside table. Next to the window was a desk and chair, and next to the door was a large, white-painted wardrobe with mirrored doors.

The whole idea of Helmersbruk and a month by the sea was starting to grow on her. Flora had always wanted wallpaper like this. The white lace curtains were pretty as well. They looked old.

It was a proper *Anne of Green Gables* room, Flora thought as she laid her red rucksack down on the crocheted bedspread. She put her hat, long scarf and jacket on the chair.

She walked over to the window and peeked out in the hope of catching sight of that manor house, but despite practically pressing her nose up against the glass, all she could see was darkness and her own reflection.

Down in the hallway, Fridolf was on his way out.

'Now I'll leave you to it. Knock if you need anything. I'm always home.'

'Thank you very much,' said Mum.

Fridolf looked up at Flora standing at the top of the stairs.

Suddenly he appeared shocked. His big blue eyes stared at Flora from under their bushy eyebrows.

'How strange...' he muttered quietly, but before Flora could ask what was so strange about her, he turned to Mum instead.

'Well then. I'm sure you'll be happy here. Many good people have lived in this house. The goodness clings to the walls. Can't you tell?'

Then he looked back at Flora again.

'Yes,' said Flora, because she really could.

She did get a good feeling about the Gatekeeper's Cottage. Maybe that was why she had already cheered up a little.

The door shut with a bang behind Fridolf. Mum giggled.

'Well, he wasn't exactly a bundle of laughs, but he seems nice enough.'

'I like him.'

'Me too. So what do you think, Flick? About the house and everything?'

'It's nice.'

'Are you sure? You think we'll be all right here?'

Mum looked a little anxious. Hardly the time to be anxious now, when it was too late to change their minds.

But Flora decided to be positive and patted Mum on the arm.

'It's going to be great!'

They tried to make themselves at home straight away. They made the beds, Mum set up her typewriter on a table in the living room and Flora lined up her school books on the desk in the room with the flowery wallpaper. She put *Anne of Green Gables* and *The Canterville Ghost* on the bedside table. There were lots of old clothes inside the wardrobe and only one empty shelf. But that was OK because Flora's clothes didn't take up much space.

'Come downstairs and let's eat,' Mum called from the kitchen.

Flora turned off the lamp in the bedroom and was just about to go downstairs when she happened to glance out the window.

Strangely enough, it was a little lighter out there now, even though it was later in the evening. Maybe the fog had dispersed and was letting the moon shine through?

Just then she saw something white flash outside the window!

And she heard a rustling sound like a whisper.

'It's her!'

The white thing disappeared too quickly for Flora to see what it was, but for a few horrible moments she thought she had seen a pale face peering in at her and whispering.

But the room was on the first floor, so surely no one could be peeking in up there?

Flora lingered in the doorway, dead still.

Did she dare go over to the window and look?

She swallowed several times.

No, she refused to be a wimp. How was she going to live in an old house for a whole month if she got scared witless every time she saw or heard something unexpected?

She walked over to the window and looked outside.

She could just about make out some tree branches in the near distance. But she couldn't see anything white.

I must have imagined it, thought Flora. *Maybe it was my own reflection?* And the sound she had thought was a whisper was probably just a branch blowing against the side of the house in the wind...

'Are you coming?' Mum called.

The smell of sausages wafted up, and Flora went downstairs.

THE MANOR HOUSE

Flora slept very badly that first night in the Gatekeeper's Cottage at Helmersbruk Manor. The mattress felt lumpy and the pillow smelt strange, even though she had brought her own bedding. The brown-yellow pattern of the bedsheets didn't match the rest of the room at all. She felt as though she should have well-ironed sheets with lace, and preferably be wearing a long white nightgown as well.

Flora looked at herself in the mirror from the bed. She didn't fit in either. She was tall for her age and had broad shoulders and a round face. Her hair was a dull in-between colour. 'Mousy', as the horsey girls called it.

Flora plaited her mousy hair in two long plaits and got out of bed. It was still dark out and the house was very cold.

In the living room Mum was sitting on the floor trying to light a fire. It wasn't going well.

'Maybe the wood is too spread out?' said Flora. 'Or too tightly packed? That doesn't work either.'

'And you're the expert, are you?' said Mum, sounding irritated. 'Where did you learn that?'

'Dad taught me,' said Flora.

Mum said nothing but even from behind she looked sad. Then suddenly a spark lit up in the fireplace.

'There!' Mum said and stood up.

It was still icy cold, so Flora put on a dark blue man's cardigan she had found hanging up in the hall. Fridolf had told Mum that they should feel free to use anything in the house. The cardigan almost came down to her knees and she wrapped it around her like a bathrobe. It was itchy and smelt like an old man but at least it was warm.

'What are you wearing? It looks like a horse blanket!' said Mum.

'The gatekeeper's Sunday best, can't you tell?'

Flora stuck her hands in the pockets of the cardigan and did a pirouette. There was something inside the right-hand pocket.

It was a little angel made of porcelain.

'Look, this was in the pocket!'

'How pretty!'

Flora inspected the porcelain figurine carefully. It was skilfully painted with careful brush strokes; the porcelain wings almost looked like they were covered in real feathers. She put the angel down on the bookshelf and suddenly a thought occurred to her.

'Mum? Did we bring the Christmas decorations?'

Mum looked up, surprised.

'The Christmas decorations? No, we didn't. We agreed we would only bring the essentials!'

'But surely Christmas decorations *are* essential! At least at Christmas.'

Mum looked sheepish.

'Yeah, I suppose so. I've just never been that into decorations myself.'

Flora knew that well enough. Mum had never been the one who decorated the Christmas tree, put out the candles or taped elves to the kitchen window. Dad, on the other hand, used to love Christmas. Decorating was his and Flora's thing.

'I'm sorry,' said Mum. 'I didn't think...'

'It doesn't matter,' Flora said, even though it wasn't true.

'Maybe we can make something ourselves? Or buy some glitter and a few elves in town?'

Flora shook her head. She didn't want new Christmas decorations. She tried not to think about the yellow cardboard box at the top of the kitchen cupboard at home, but the more she tried not to, the more she thought about the box and everything in it.

The silver tinsel that was a bit thin in places but still pretty, the red-painted wooden candlesticks, the star-shaped paper lantern, the ugly elves she had made out of wool when she was little.

But most of all, she thought about the little light brown box with those delicate old glass baubles that had once belonged to her grandmother.

Every year on Christmas Eve Dad would carefully lift the baubles out of their bed of tissue paper and say: 'We'll hang these on the sturdiest branches, because these were my mother's prized possessions...'

He would always say those exact words and it was in that moment that Flora started to feel like it was really, *really* Christmas.

Last Christmas, which turned out to be Dad's last, he had been so weak that he could barely get out of his chair, but he managed to gather enough strength to hang the first bauble, then let Flora take care of the rest.

Flora turned her face away so that Mum wouldn't see the tears she couldn't hold back. No Christmas decorations, no special baubles, no Dad. Just a sad little porcelain angel on a bookshelf. That was probably about as Christmassy as it was going to get.

'I'm going out,' she said.

'Have fun,' said Mum.

It was nice to get out into the fresh air. It was less windy than before but still just as overcast and grey.

Flora pulled on her white woolly gloves with pompoms and let out a breath that misted in the air. From the front steps she could see a glimpse of the sea, which was just as grey as everything else.

Next to the cottage she could also see the gate that the gatekeeper would have once guarded. It was one of those wide double gates made of swirling black cast iron, with two latches fastened in the centre. Right at the top, in the middle of the ornate patterns, was a large letter H. It must have been gold once but now it was flaking and dull.

H for Helmersbruk, thought Flora. Or what had Fridolf said it was called? The von Hiems manor? Maybe the H stood for Hiems then? What a mysterious name.

She walked over and touched the gate, but it wouldn't budge. She supposed the only way in was through the smaller gate in the wall, which they had used yesterday.

Flora looked around for Fridolf's Washhouse but couldn't see any buildings other than the Gatekeeper's Cottage. Somewhere behind the blanket of clouds, the sun must have been rising. It was getting brighter.

Inside the wall it was like a long-forgotten park. The bushes and trees looked overgrown, but it was clear that everything had been planted with care once upon a time.

Flora walked around a prickly bush and found herself at the end of a long avenue of tall trees. The trees had lost their leaves but the canopy branches were so dense that they grew together at the top and made the avenue look like a tunnel. The road ahead was bumpy and full of muddy puddles, so she had to watch her step.

Flora walked, hopped, and tiptoed forward, careful where she put her feet. She soon realized that she probably should have worn boots instead of canvas shoes, but there was no point in going back and changing them now. She was already muddy up to her knees.

There was a rustling in the trees above her. A gust of wind swept through the avenue. It was a strangely warm breeze that grabbed at Flora's plaits and scarf.

And, stranger still, the wind whispered! It was just like the whisper she'd heard outside her window the night before.

It's her! She's back!

Flora stopped in her tracks and looked around. Who said that? There wasn't a soul to be seen.

What she could see, however, was the von Hiems mansion for the first time.

Flora was so taken aback that she immediately forgot all about whispering voices, wet feet and everything else besides.

Never in her life had Flora seen such an incredible house. She stood perfectly still for a long time, staring and staring.

The house was three storeys high with a pointed roof and all sorts of balconies and bays jutting out here and there. There were windows in all shapes and sizes: round, square, oval, big and small. Just like the outer wall and the Gatekeeper's Cottage, the mansion was built of brick, and in one corner was a small turret and a wall covered almost entirely with some sort of creeper plant. Some of the windows had diamond-shaped panes of stained glass, others had been boarded up completely.

It was clear that no one had lived there for a very, very long time.

She almost felt like crying at the sight of this beautiful manor house in all its dilapidated, majestic glory.

Did she dare go closer? What if—her heart leapt—what if the door wasn't locked and she could just go in and have a look? Not take anything, not even touch anything, just look around...

She took one step forward then stopped. It felt very bold to walk straight up and open the door. Maybe she should walk around the house first to see it from different angles?

Walking around the house turned out to be easier said than done. She had to find her way through a grove of overgrown trees and very nearly fell into an old fountain. Then she had to scramble through several dense bushes, over a low wall and round a mossy statue of a half-naked woman holding a pot.

But it was worth it because the back of the building was even more magnificent than the front! A porch with beautiful windows looked out on to a large garden with lots of statues and platforms of various heights. Roses and sculpted bushes must have grown there once, she had no doubt. What a wonderful sight it must have been! Real manor grounds, with a rose garden and everything!

Above the porch was a large balcony with tall doors that probably led to a great hall of some sort. A ballroom maybe? Or was it only fairytale palaces that had ballrooms?

Flora walked further away to see the whole building from a distance, then went closer again to get a better look at the details.

How old might this mansion be? Definitely very old, several hundred years. Why didn't people build houses like this any more? With all its beautiful windows and its pointed metal roof, it was so much more elegant than typical square blocks of ugly flats.

Who owned this estate? she wondered. *It couldn't be Fridolf, or why would he live in a washhouse? No, Fridolf must be some sort of caretaker,* Flora thought.

Maybe a relative of the von Hiems who had built the manor was still alive today? If so, they must own it all, the lucky devil.

But then why did no one live there now? Sure, the house was rather dilapidated, but if it belonged to her, she would gladly put up with a bit of wear and tear. Especially that turret–imagine having that as a bedroom!

It was bizarre, but straight away Flora had a strong sense that she loved every inch of this old house. It was a cold morning, but she felt all warm inside. Was this what it felt like to fall in love? Was it strange to fall in love with a place before ever falling in love with a person?

If so, then I am strange, thought Flora.

The grounds turned out to be bigger than Flora had first thought. The park gradually gave way to woodland, so it was hard to say where the manor's estate ended. One day she would walk a little further and see if there was anything exciting in the woods as well.

After walking slowly around the whole manor she found herself back in the courtyard at the end of the avenue.

A staircase led up to a massive door made of dark wood. There was an oval-shaped window in the door that looked to her like a stern eye. It actually sort of felt like the manor was watching Flora approach. She felt shy.

'Um... hello. I don't mean to disturb you, I just wanted a little look around.'

How silly, standing there talking to an old house. What if the horsey girls could see her now? But that eye-window made her feel like saying hello was the polite thing to do.

She went up the steps, put her hand on the large door handle and tried to push it down.

The door was locked.

Of course.

Flora sighed with disappointment. She was simply dying to go inside! She was weak-kneed with curiosity. Should she go back around and try the porch door? Or maybe she could open one of these windows?

Suddenly she heard some music.

A faint melody was playing somewhere nearby!

She recognized the tune. It was a gentle tinkling version of *Oh Christmas Tree*. It didn't sound like someone playing an instrument, but more like a music box.

But where could the music box be in that case? It sounded like the music was coming from inside the house, but that didn't make any sense. The house was locked up and deserted, and surely a music box needed someone to wind it up.

Flora took a step back and looked around, suddenly suspicious. What if someone was trying to trick or frighten her?

Flora was used to that sort of thing. Dead spiders in her desk, rotten apples in her school bag, the lights being switched off when she was showering after gym class. The horsey girls never gave up, and there was nothing she could do except fumble through the darkness for the light switch to the sound of a delighted choir of giggles outside.

'Better wash that muck off, Filthy Flora!'

'Here are some pet spiders that can live in your hair.'

'Spiders like living in mouse nests, ha ha...'

In that moment, standing on the steps of the von Hiems manor house, hundreds of miles from school and the horsey girls, Flora made a promise to herself.

She spoke it out loud in a determined voice:

'Nothing in Helmersbruk is going to scare me.'

She certainly wasn't going to be scared of whispering voices, pale faces or music boxes tinkling in an abandoned house.

She looked defiantly along the avenue.

Anyone trying to frighten Flora Winter was going to be sorely disappointed. End of story.

The music stopped.

THE SHEPHERD

Flora stood on the doorstep and listened awhile longer, but the music box had gone quiet.

Maybe I'm actually just losing my marbles, she thought.

After all, this was the third time within twenty-four hours that she had seen or heard something and not been sure whether it was real or a figment of her imagination.

The whispers, the face outside the bedroom window, the feeling that the manor house was watching her. But this music had continued for some time and sounded very real.

Maybe this was just how it was in old places? Maybe events of the past had a sort of... echo, even though the people who had lived there were long gone?

A cold shiver ran down Flora's spine, but it wasn't an unpleasant feeling. She had decided not to be afraid, after all. She was more intrigued.

Could the house be trying to tell me something? she thought, caressing the locked door with her gloved hand. *What if the von Hiems manor has a secret it wants to share with me?*

She laughed a little at the thought. It was silly, but at the same time gloriously exciting. What if Filthy Flora with the mousy hair had some sort of magical connection to this incredible house? What a dream come true that would be!

When she turned around to leave she caught sight of something. Close to the building's facade was what must have once been a flower bed. Now the ground was covered with withered grass and moss, but she also spied something lushly green.

Flora knelt down by the flower bed. She pulled off her gloves and dug through the wilting grass. A green bud was trying to push its way up into the light. Flora didn't know there were plants that grew in December. Did the poor little thing think it was spring already?

Then she saw another bud, and another! In fact, there was a whole host of buds defying the cold and dark. Growing against all odds.

Flora started to pull dried grass away to help the little plants along. What were they? Crocuses? No, they had rounder buds...

I live here in the manor, she thought. *I am Miss Flora. Everybody loves me. I have an enormous wardrobe full of beautiful clothes and a maid who brushes and plaits my hair every day. My room is at the top of the turret and I have bookshelves from floor to ceiling—I need a ladder to reach the ones at the top. I always wear a long white nightdress to bed, and every morning I wake up, throw open the window and gaze out at the sea glittering beyond the blooming garden.*

Daydreaming came easily in a place like this. Flora had never really felt like she belonged in the present day. She didn't get the music or TV shows that her classmates were into. She didn't especially like modern clothes either. T-shirts with prints, jeans and all that. Flora would have preferred to wear dresses with puffy sleeves, like in *Anne of Green Gables*. But if she did, the horsey girls would probably kill themselves laughing.

Flora was lonely. She hadn't always been. She'd had a best friend only a couple of years ago.

Johanna.

When they were little, Johanna and Flora looked almost identical and often pretended they were sisters. When Johanna got dungarees for Christmas, Flora begged Mum for a pair exactly the same; when Flora started wearing her hair in plaits, Johanna wanted to as well.

Johanna thought that Flora made up the best stories, and they would often act out the little plays that Flora wrote. They also used to go to the cinema, make chocolate treats together, and talk about everything under the sun. They had a lot of secrets from everybody else, but none from each other.

Flora had taken it for granted that she and Johanna would be best friends forever. But then in Year 6 Johanna started taking horse-riding lessons. Flora couldn't join her because her parents said it was much too expensive. Dad was already too sick to work, and Mum was writing as much as she possibly could, but they just didn't have the money for riding lessons.

Then one thing led to another.

Johanna didn't have time to go to Flora's after school any more; she went to the stables instead. On the weekends there were gymkhanas and in the summer holidays Johanna went to riding camp. When Johanna did agree to play with Flora, everything was wrong. Johanna didn't want to act out plays any more or listen to Flora's stories. She wanted to talk about horses, and it was difficult for Flora to keep track of all the stirrups, halters and bridles. It was pretty boring too.

By the time they started Year 7, Johanna had gone to the same riding camp as two girls in another class at school, and suddenly they were all best friends.

Flora wasn't welcome. On the contrary, the horsey girls thought that Flora was a total loser.

Johanna was never the one who said really nasty things to Flora, but she didn't stick up for her either. She laughed out loud when the others came out with mean insults.

Don't you ever wash, Filthy Flora? Freaky Flora. Ugh, what smells so bad? Fishy Flora!

When Flora had come back to school for the first time after Dad's death it seemed like Johanna wanted to say something. She gave Flora funny looks, but she didn't come over to talk to her. And the other horsey girls laughed at Flora for wearing Dad's chunky watch on her wrist. She had put it on that morning because it made her feel better to have a little piece of Dad with her now that he was gone. But the watch was too big and kept slipping off, so finally she put it in her rucksack instead.

With time, Flora got used to being alone. She didn't even miss Johanna—the old Johanna—that much any more. And she didn't have many opportunities to make new friends. She could do without.

Besides, she had her own imagination. And she never grew tired of that.

I, Miss Flora, have a cook with rosy cheeks, and servants, a chauffeur, a gatekeeper and a gardener. But I have magical green fingers also and can make flowers grow, even in midwinter. So the head gardener says, 'It's probably best if Miss Flora tends to the flower bed at the front of the house herself,' and I am happy to. Soon it will be

Christmas and the servants will bring a huge fir tree into the house and put it up in the ballroom, like they always do.

She was reminded of the old Christmas baubles lying in their box back in the city. Grandma's prized possessions. Those old-fashioned glass baubles would have been perfect for a Christmas tree in the von Hiems mansion.

She shut her eyes and pictured what the ballroom would have looked like on Christmas Eve. Thick crimson velvet drapes hanging from the tall windows, a shiny parquet floor, a crackling fire, and in the middle of the room, a huge Christmas tree covered in beautiful glass ornaments, tissue paper and real candles...

Suddenly her fingertips came upon something hard. She opened her eyes again. Something was hidden underneath the earth. Some sort of root, maybe?

It was difficult to get a grip on it but eventually she managed to pry it up.

She rubbed the object with her glove.

It was a little man made of porcelain. How had he got into the flower bed?

Flora's legs had gone to sleep from crouching for so long. She had no idea what time it was. Her fingers were almost purple with cold and her stomach growled. It was probably time to take a break.

She took a step back to view the results of her morning's work. She had tidied several metres of the flower bed, but there was still a lot left to do.

The little buds were pointing straight up to the sky and their pale green colour made all the greyness around feel a little cheerier. Flora thought the buds almost looked bigger now than they had when she first started, as if they had actually grown while she'd been daydreaming.

I'll need a pair of gardening gloves, Flora thought, *and a little rake as well. Maybe Fridolf could lend me some gardening tools?*

She looked up at the manor house.

'I'll be back soon.'

She squelched her way down the avenue, barely bothering to avoid the muddy puddles seeing as she was already dirty and wet.

Just to the right of the gate with the big letter H she saw a little brick house peeking out from behind a spruce tree. That must be the Washhouse.

I'll just pop in on Fridolf quickly, she thought.

The light was on inside the little house and Flora heard the sound of a woman's voice. Did Fridolf have a visitor? Then she realized it was the radio.

She knocked and, finding the door unlocked, went inside.

'Hello?'

Fridolf was sitting at a table with a teacup in front of him. He held up a finger.

'Shh. Weather report.'

Flora stood in the doorway for quite a long time until the voice on the radio said, 'That was the weather,' and lively orchestra music started to play.

'Night frost, but no snow at least,' Fridolf said, sounding pleased.

Flora thought it was nice to have snow at Christmas but nodded as if she agreed.

'Was there something you wanted?' he asked.

Flora put her hand in her glove and took out the porcelain man.

'I found this up at the big house. Did you drop it?'

Fridolf made no movement to take the figurine, so Flora put it on the table. Fridolf sat quietly for a while and just looked at it.

'Well, I'll be...' he said at last. 'The little shepherd seems to have wandered off somehow.'

'Shepherd?'

'Aye. See the crook in his hand? And there's a lamb by his feet.'

Flora leant closer to the figurine to take a proper look. Fridolf was right. The paint had faded but now she could see the crook and the lamb.

'So what should I do with it?' Flora asked. 'Maybe someone is missing it.'

'There's none left here to miss him. You've found him, you keep him.'

'OK.'

Flora put the shepherd back into her glove and lingered, unsure whether she had the nerve to ask more questions. Fridolf didn't exactly seem chatty.

'The Gatekeeper's Cottage is lovely,' she said.

'Mm. Were you cold last night?'

'Maybe a little.'

'There's more firewood round the back of the house.'

'Aha. Great. The manor is nice too. Beautiful, really.'

Fridolf grunted and it was hard to tell whether or not he agreed.

'Um, there was something I wanted to ask you...' Flora continued gingerly. 'I was wondering if I might be allowed to tidy up that flower bed up by the big house?'

'Oh? For a school project?'

'Yes,' she said, even though it wasn't true.

The old man looked at her with that same surprised, curious expression again. Had it been such a strange question? Then he shrugged.

'Go ahead. For all the good it'll do.'
'Might you have a spade or rake you could lend me?'
'No,' said Fridolf. 'The orangery is probably your best bet.'
'What's an orangey?'
'Orang-e-ry. Posh word for greenhouse.'
'Oh.'

Flora wanted to ask Fridolf about the von Hiems mansion. Who had lived there? Was there a ballroom inside? What was in the turret? Could she go inside and take a look?

But Fridolf seemed to think they had been talking for long enough. He raised his finger again and turned to the radio.

'News now.'

A voice started talking about prime ministers and invasions. Flora waved silently and left. She could always come back another day.

But now she was ravenously hungry.

The blanket of yellow-grey clouds was thinning and suddenly a little gap opened up, allowing a ray of sunshine to break through. The sunlight seemed to bring everything it touched to life. The H shone on the metal gates, the leaves on the bushes shone as if covered in Christmas decorations, and a sudden flash almost blinded Flora as she walked.

Something reflected the sunlight directly into her face. But then the clouds closed up again and the ray of light disappeared.

Could it have been a bit of broken glass? Best to make sure, so that no one would step on it.

The grass beneath Flora's feet was sodden and brown. She walked carefully so as not to tread on the piece of glass, or whatever it was. Then she saw something in the grass near her left foot.

It was a pair of glasses. They looked old but intact, with brown metal frames and small lenses. Flora pulled off her gloves and picked them up.

She was so surprised that she dropped the glasses on the grass again.

'What? How in the?...'

The glasses were warm!

As warm as if someone had just taken them off a second ago and laid them directly in Flora's hand.

THE SNOW-WHITE SQUIRREL

Flora could hear the clacking of the typewriter from all the way out in the garden. Mum was sitting in the living room with ruddy cheeks and messy hair. She didn't even notice Flora come in.

'Hello,' Flora said gently so as not to startle her, but Mum jumped anyway.

'Holy moly, you scared me! Everything OK, Flick?'

'Mm. What's for lunch?'

'What? Lunch? Um... could you make yourself a sandwich?'

Mum had a wild look about her. Her fringe was sticking straight up in the air and her eyes were wide and slightly bloodshot. She always got like this when she was writing; she forgot about everything else around her. Dad and Flora used to laugh at Mum when she disappeared into her writing bubble.

'We should try to feed Mum some dinner,' Dad would joke. 'If we're careful she might not even notice us stuffing a couple of meatballs in her mouth while she's writing...'

Now Flora had no one to joke with, but she was glad that Mum was getting along with her book. It was better to see her writing than crying. Mum always tried to cry in secret but it didn't work. Flora always knew.

When Flora saw the little angel on the bookshelf it occurred to her that it was about the same size as the shepherd she had found in the flower bed. She fished him out of her glove and put him next to the angel.

Yes indeed. They looked like they belonged together. They both seemed to be painted in the same style, though the shepherd was still a little mucky from lying in the soil.

She took the glasses out of her pocket as well and examined them carefully. They were cool now.

Whose could they be? They looked small. She couldn't imagine Fridolf wearing them.

Flora stood in front of the hallway mirror and tried on the glasses. Gosh, they made everything very big and blurry. They must belong to someone near-sighted.

Maybe she could put up a notice in the gardens. *Found: glasses. Come to the Gatekeeper's Cottage.*

That was a good idea.

But first she needed food. She put the glasses on the window sill in the kitchen, made two big sandwiches and brought one to Mum.

'Eat,' she said.

'Mm? Yes, of course... thanks.'

Flora took her sandwich up to her room. She changed into dry trousers and socks, wrapped the gatekeeper's cardigan around herself and sat down at the desk.

The clattering of the typewriter continued downstairs. Mum had really got into the swing of writing.

Flora took a bite of her sandwich and absent-mindedly tapped the tabletop with a biro.

She was in a funny mood. She couldn't decide whether she was happy or sad. Maybe a little of both.

She had had a wonderful morning at the manor, but whenever she returned from her fantasy worlds, all the sorrows of reality remained.

Most of all, she missed Dad. It was like a blister that refused to heal. She could forget about the pain briefly but as soon as she moved it would blaze again.

She was sleepy too. She had slept badly the night before and been out all morning. Her school books were lying by the window, but they didn't appeal to her at all.

Maybe I should take a nap, like old folks and little kids do? Flora thought.

She would have plenty of time for schoolwork later. There was no TV in the Gatekeeper's Cottage, so there wasn't much to do in the evenings. Surely there was nothing to stop Flora from doing her homework in the evening? That way she could spend all day outside while there was daylight. Mum was barely aware of what was happening around her when she wrote, so she was unlikely to protest.

Flora lay down on the crocheted bedspread and looked drowsily at the window. Would she have time to go back to the flower bed today? It would start getting dark soon and she hadn't gone out looking for that greenhouse yet.

On the other hand, there was no rush. They were going to live here for a whole month, after all. She would probably have time to sort out the flower bed and go on all sorts of adventures around the von Hiems estate. It was probably best to take it a little at a time, like enjoying a bag of sweets slowly instead of scoffing them all down straight away.

The sound of the typewriter was soothing and the bobbles of the bedspread felt nice through her clothes, sort of like a back scratcher.

Flora shut her eyes and breathed deeply. Her mind was racing; she had a lot to think about.

The porcelain shepherd in the flower bed, the angel in the cardigan pocket, the glasses on the lawn... would she find more things in the gardens?

Who had lost them? Or was someone putting them there for Flora to find? And what about the music box? The one that had played *Oh Christmas Tree* inside the locked manor house.

Did these objects have a connection to the music box? Were they some sort of clue? If so, to what?

Even though her eyes were closed she could clearly see the garden and avenue in front of her.

And now she was walking, no, gliding over the ground, moving closer and closer to the mansion.

The eye-shaped window was watching her, and she heard someone whisper:

'What is the meaning of this?'

'Can't you see? That's not her!' said another voice.

'Let her in and we'll take a closer look,' said a third.

The hefty door swung open, soft and quiet like a curtain.

Flora floated into the building.

A long dark staircase, paintings, furniture, mirrors–no, no! It was all going too fast, she didn't have enough time to look at everything properly... further now, up the stairs and there, straight ahead she saw tall double doors with light shining through the cracks and the music box playing *Oh Christmas Tree* very loudly, and the music went faster and faster, and eager voices whispered over each other:

'Come into the great hall, then we'll see, come closer if you are who we think you are...'

'But she mustn't think she can find the treasure.'

'No, the treasure is ours.'

'Ours, all ours, not hers...'

Flora sat up in bed with a yelp. She was gasping for breath and her heart was thudding as quickly as Mum's typewriter downstairs. The dream had felt so real that she was genuinely surprised to find herself back in her bedroom in the Gatekeeper's Cottage.

Then she saw something outside the window! Something white sitting on a tree branch and looking at her with watchful little red eyes.

It was a squirrel.

A snow-white squirrel.

They sat perfectly still on either side of the windowpane and stared at each other, Flora and the small creature.

Flora had never seen anything like it. She knew that some animals changed colour for winter to be able to camouflage better with the snow, but she had never seen a pure white squirrel before. Especially not one with red eyes.

Then Flora smiled, realizing that this must have been the white thing that flashed outside the window the night before and frightened her.

Not a spooky white face after all, but a cute little squirrel.

'Hello there, Snow Squirrel,' she whispered. 'You gave me a fright yesterday.'

The squirrel almost looked offended, then it turned around, hopped on to another branch and disappeared.

Flora got up from the bed and tried to see where the squirrel had gone but it was nowhere to be seen. The daylight was fading. She wouldn't have time to look for the greenhouse today; the grounds were huge and she could easily get lost in the dark.

I'll do it tomorrow, as soon as the sun is up, Flora decided and went downstairs.

'Have you ever seen a snow-white squirrel?' she asked her mother.

'Mm,' said Mum, still writing.

Flora saw that she had eaten her sandwich. That was good.

'What are we going to have for dinner?'

'Sorry, what? Oh yes, dinner.'

Mum sighed, pulled a sheet of paper out of the typewriter and fed in another.

'We should really go to the shop. But we could probably make do with what we have.'

'All right,' said Flora. 'What do we have?'

'Sausage stroganoff.'

Flora couldn't help but sigh. Sausage, sausage and more sausage.

'Can't we eat anything other than sausage?'

Mum's eyes looked surprised behind her large glasses.

'Like what?'

'I don't know, potato pancakes, for example.'

'Potato pancakes? What in the world? How would you even make them?'

Flora rolled her eyes.

'You grate potatoes and mix it up with milk and egg and fry it in a frying pan.'

Mum's glasses slipped down to the tip of her nose.

'Did you learn that at school?'

Flora shrugged her shoulders.

'No. It was only an idea. We can have sausages again.'

Flora was a little confused herself. Potato pancakes. Where had that idea come from? She couldn't remember ever having eaten such a thing, so how did she know the recipe?

The fire was dying and Flora noticed that the wood basket was empty.

'We're out of firewood.'

'Oh dear. Could you fetch some? There should be a woodshed outside.'

'OK.'

Flora picked up the wood basket and carried it into the hall. She wedged her feet into Mum's boots, which, unlike her shoes, were warm and dry.

It was twilight. Quiet too, without even a whisper of sea breeze.

The wood basket wasn't particularly heavy but it was very awkward to carry. She probably wouldn't be able to carry much wood in it, but maybe she could fill it up in several trips.

Hearing a scratching sound nearby, Flora turned around eagerly, hoping to catch sight of the squirrel. But there was no snow-white squirrel to be seen.

She still hadn't managed to shake off that strange dream from her nap. Usually Flora didn't remember her dreams. Except for those wonderful dreams that made waking up horrible. The ones in which Dad was alive and well, happy and healthy and everything was like before. Being wrenched out of those dreams and remembering that he was gone never got any less devastating.

But she had actually gone inside the manor house in this dream. Now she was even more curious about what it looked like inside for real. Would it be anything like her dream?

How creepy that would be!

Mum often praised Flora for her active imagination.

'You're going to be a writer as well. It comes easily to us daydreamers.'

But what use was an active imagination when the thoughts spinning inside her head only confused her? Like those whispering voices in her dream. What were they about? Had Flora made them up? They sounded so real...

Flora tried to budge the basket that she had filled with logs from the neat woodshed by the wall. It was ridiculously heavy and she had to tug with all her might.

There was that scratching sound again! Flora put down the basket, stood up straight and tried to figure out where it was coming from.

There was no one there except her, neither human nor animal.

She lugged the basket back to the door of the Gatekeeper's Cottage. She paused to catch her breath at the bottom of the steps—and saw someone standing outside the gate!

A solitary person stood there, perfectly still, looking in through the swirling iron.

Had they seen Flora? She didn't think so. They seemed to be looking up at the manor.

In the half-light she couldn't tell for sure whether it was a man or a woman, but Flora got the feeling it was a woman. The figure was wearing a duffel coat with a hood, and had long, thin legs.

Should I say something? Flora thought. *It might be a friend of Fridolf's who doesn't know how to get in.*

Just then the door to the Gatekeeper's Cottage opened and Mum peered out.

'Poor little Flick, that basket is much too heavy for you. Wait, let me help you.'

Flora turned back to the gate. The hooded figure had vanished.

THE LABYRINTH

Flora woke up the next morning disappointed. She hadn't had any dreams all night. Part of her was hoping her dream from yesterday's nap might continue. Even though she had woken up with her heart in her throat, it had been so exciting to dream her way into the von Hiems manor.

She wondered what lay behind those tall double doors at the top of the long dark staircase. Why was light shining through the gaps? But she would rather not hear those annoying whispering voices again.

It looked like a nice day, at least. The sun hadn't risen yet, but the sky was clear and the branches outside Flora's bedroom window were covered in crisp hoarfrost. That snow-white squirrel could easily camouflage itself today among all that whiteness. She decided she was going to find the greenhouse, continue her work in the flower beds and maybe have another go at getting into the house. Lying in bed and hoping to dream her way into a building seemed a bit silly when the actual building was only a short walk away.

Mum wasn't up yet so Flora went down to the living room and laid a few logs on the fire. The flames came to life at once. As if she'd been lighting fires in a cold old house every morning of her life.

The cupboards were more or less bare so she supposed they would have to go shopping in Helmersbruk today. Flora buttered some bread and sat down to eat it by the fire because the kitchen was too cold.

Eating breakfast like this wasn't so bad. The fire crackled cheerfully and warmed her feet. She leant back in the armchair and took a look around the room.

The gatekeeper had clearly been an avid reader. The shelves were filled with old books. Most were in languages that Flora didn't understand. There were a few little cross-stitch pictures of flowers on the wall and a vase of dried geraniums on the window sill.

Did the gatekeeper have a wife? Did she make those pictures? Or did the wife read the books while the gatekeeper did the handicrafts? Either way, it was a cosy home.

If I lived in this house for real, I wouldn't change a thing, thought Flora. *Well, maybe I'd get a TV. But the furniture and decorations are much nicer than the things we have in the city.*

Mum's typewriter was next to Flora. It had paper in it, as though Mum had taken a break mid-chapter.

Flora wasn't usually all that interested in her mother's work, but she took a glance at what she had written. There were already several complicated words in the first lines.

'Class society.'

'Oppressive culture.'

'Bourgeoisie.' Wasn't that a type of disgusting beef stew with pickled onions in it? No, that was something else.

All around the typewriter were piles of paper, notes and

binders. No wonder their bags were so heavy if this is what Mum considered to be 'the essentials'.

Flora finished her breakfast and ran back up to her room to get dressed.

'You're awfully chipper for this time in the morning,' Mum muttered as she emerged from the bathroom.

'I'm going out!'

She had to be quick, or Mum might realize they needed to go shopping. Flora was aching to get out into her garden. They could just as easily go into Helmersbruk a little later.

It looked set to be a cold day, so Flora put on two pairs of trousers and a thick polo neck under the gatekeeper's special cardigan and her jacket. She couldn't find her hat anywhere, but luckily her scarf was long enough to wrap around her neck and head. Now she was so padded that her arms stuck straight out and she had to turn her whole body if she wanted to look to the sides. But at least she wouldn't be cold.

Suddenly she felt a pang of worry. How had the shoots in the flower bed outside the house fared in the cold? What if they had frozen?

She hurried over to the manor house. The grass crunched beneath her feet and the sky was the colour of apricots. The glittering white gardens were unbelievably beautiful in the pinky-orange light. It looked like a completely different landscape from the previous day when everything had been grey.

When Flora first caught a glimpse of the manor house, she thought she saw light shining out of some of the windows and stopped dead.

Then she realized it was only the reflection of the sunrise in the windowpanes.

The manor looked so alive in the sunlight. The eye-window in the door seemed less stern today too. Flora waved to the eye as she scurried past.

'Hello, it's me again.'

The shoots in the bed where she had weeded the previous day looked like they were doing very well, despite the cold. They had actually grown overnight. Some now had short stalks and small buds covered in velvety down. The buds were green but what colour would the flowers be? White or red or another colour altogether? Oh, how she hoped to see the flowers bloom before their month at Helmersbruk was up.

Flora's fingers were itching to carry on working in the flower bed, but it was far too cold a day to sit still scratching around in the earth with bare fingers. She would need tools. She set out to find the orangery.

Flora walked briskly towards the western gable of the house. She had no idea where the orangery was, but she had to start looking somewhere. She had walked around the house the previous day but had been so busy admiring the building itself that she hadn't kept an eye out for orangeries or other outbuildings. Surely the greenhouse would be close by.

The manor residents probably grew lots of special flowers to pick and display in vases when they threw parties.

If this were my manor, I would put the orangery somewhere over there, thought Flora.

She had to struggle through a rather spiky thicket of bushes to get to where she wanted to go. On the other side, an overgrown lawn almost the size of a football field was spread out before her. The only thing growing there besides grass was a row of tall hedges, like a green wall completely blocking her view beyond it.

Could the orangery be behind this hedge-wall?

Flora crossed the lawn surrounded by a cloud of vapour every time she exhaled. She breathed deeply and felt the cold, fresh air spreading throughout her body.

Miss Flora is going to visit her orangery today.

She giggled to herself thinking that all her layers of jumpers and scarves were hardly what the mistress of the manor would have worn in the olden days. But it didn't matter.

The orangery is my pride and joy. Inside it I have grown the most beautiful flowers imaginable. In spring there will be flowers in every shade of yellow. In summer I prefer pink and pale blue. In autumn I want everything to be orange, like the sky now, and in winter, well obviously only blood-red and snow-white will do.

What did people grow in greenhouses in the olden days? Roses? Peonies?

Dad used to be really good at identifying flowers. His mother, Flora's grandmother, who had died long before Flora was born, had worked as a florist. Back when Dad was still healthy, he often brought home bouquets for Mum and named every individual flower.

'Snapdragon, dahlia, prairie rose,' he would say.

Mum considered flowers an unnecessary expense.

'The only flower I want is this one,' she would say and give Flora a hug.

Of course, the name Flora meant flower. Flora wished she had listened more carefully when Dad used to name the different flowers in the bouquets. It would be cool to know lots of plant names.

There was a huge greenhouse in the city with a pond filled with water lilies, some of which had leaves big enough to sit on.

Was the von Hiems orangery big enough for a water-lily pond? Flora was getting more and more excited with every step.

The manor house is filled with silver buckets of fresh flowers. And they never run out because I am so green-fingered that new flowers grow quicker than the old ones can wither. It's like magic!

She came to the wall of hedges in the middle of the lawn. She was sure she would see this orangery soon. But when she walked around, expecting to see what was on the other side, she became confused. The hedges just carried on around the corner, and when she tried to turn the next corner, the same thing happened again.

This wasn't a wall at all, but an enormous square of green hedges!

How strange. Why on earth would anyone plant them like this?

When Flora rounded the third corner she caught sight of a small opening. There was a wooden gate standing ajar in the hedge-wall. Beyond it Flora saw a narrow path lined with even more hedges.

Now Flora understood what she was looking at.

It was a labyrinth, of course!

She had heard of such things but never really understood what the point in them was. Planting hedges in the shape of a labyrinth and letting them grow so high that people had to wander around inside and not know how to get out. Did people in the olden days think that getting lost was fun? Flora didn't think so, and she had no intention of going into the labyrinth.

No, she would continue to search for the greenhouse instead.

She turned back to face the manor and looked around. There was the manor house, the rose garden, and a little further away was a patch of woodland. She couldn't see any other buildings from here, but it looked like there was a little path that disappeared into the trees. She could always follow that and see where it led.

But no sooner had she taken a couple of steps in that direction than something startled her and made her freeze.

There it was again!

The music! The music box playing *Oh Christmas Tree*.

Flora spun around and tried to figure out where the music was coming from. She was pretty far away from the manor house, so if it was the same music box as yesterday, then someone must have moved it.

The music box was out there somewhere, not far from the very spot where Flora was standing.

Slowly, she turned around.

Yes, it was just as she had suspected.

The music was coming from the labyrinth.

For a few moments, she almost forgot to breathe. What should she do?

Was someone trying to lure her in? She wasn't that easily fooled.

But at the same time, she was burning with curiosity. What was in there? Was it really a music box playing that tune? What did it look like? And who had wound it up? Fridolf? Unlikely.

There must have been someone else in the grounds.

Flora slowly walked closer to the entrance of the labyrinth. It would be foolish to go in alone. What if she couldn't find her way out again? How long would it take before Mum started to wonder where she was? Certainly several hours, and even longer if Mum was busy writing. Would Mum or Fridolf hear Flora if she got lost and had to shout for help?

'Hello? Is anybody in there?' she called but no answer came.

All was quiet but for that same tinkling melody playing over and over again.

Perhaps she could climb a tree to get a look at the labyrinth from above? It might not be all that complicated. Flora looked around but the only nearby tree didn't look very climb-friendly.

The melody was playing louder and faster now. Flora started singing along absent-mindedly.

'*O Tannenbaum, o Tannenbaum, wie treu sind deine Blätter...*'

Right, I'm going in, Flora made up her mind and touched the gate. But in the very next second she regretted it and withdrew her hand.

No, this isn't a good idea. What do I care about a silly old music box stuck on a loop? I'm going now, to the orangery.

She set her sights on the little path into the grove of trees, but just as she was about to take her first step, she heard a voice behind her say:

'Oh, those blasted spectacles, where can they be?'

EGON

Who had spoken? Flora turned around so fast that she almost lost her balance.

A tall boy was standing near her on the lawn. How had she not heard him approach?

He was dressed in a green flat cap and knitted jumper and looked a little older than her. Maybe even high school age.

He looked just as surprised to see her as she was to see him.

'Goodness me, I do beg your pardon, miss!' he said. 'I thought you were someone else.'

Flora cleared her throat, unsure at first whether she could even get a word out, but she did in the end.

'Did you say that you'd lost your spectacles?' she stuttered.

'Yes, it is most irksome. I cannot fathom where they could have got to this time. I have searched everywhere.'

'Did they have brown frames and round lenses?'

He laughed.

'Yes, as do all spectacles, I'm sure. Have you seen them?'

Flora nodded.

'Yes! I found a pair of glasses by a tree down by the gate. I'll go and fetch them.'

Just then she felt warmth inside her jacket pocket. She felt heat against her leg and, puzzled, stuck her hand in her pocket to find out what it was.

It was the glasses!

Flora was sure she had left them on the window sill in the Gatekeeper's Cottage, but she must have been so spaced out that she had somehow managed to put them back in her pocket before going out again.

'There they are!' the boy said happily. 'What luck! Father says I'm as blind as a mole without them, and he's probably right...'

He took the glasses from Flora and put them on. They suited him. He looked at Flora and smiled widely.

'How odd.'

'What's odd?'

'You bear a striking resemblance. Hardly surprising that I mistook you for her.'

'For who?'

'A friend of mine. But how terribly improper of me to not have introduced myself. My name is Egon.'

He had such a funny way of talking, sort of formal and old-fashioned. Flora wasn't sure how to respond. Should she talk back to him like a character in an old book or should she just be normal? Was this how all high school students in Helmersbruk spoke or was this boy trying to stand out?

'My name's Flora.'

Egon bowed slightly and for a few confused seconds Flora wondered whether she should curtsy, but decided against it. That would be going too far.

'Were you on your way into the labyrinth, Miss Flora?'

'No. Or... I don't think so. But I heard music.'

'Is that so? How curious.'

They stood quietly and listened for a few moments but the music box had stopped playing.

'Is it difficult to find your way through the labyrinth?' asked Flora. 'Have you tried?'

Egon nodded.

'I've made many attempts and have come to the conclusion that it is impossible. At least, I have never found the centre.'

'What's in the centre?'

'Not having been there, I couldn't say. But that is always the way with labyrinths. One must find the way to the centre and then back out again.'

'I see.'

Flora turned back to face the labyrinth and peeked in through the entrance. It couldn't be all that far to the centre, but apparently it was difficult to find. Something about this maze was calling to her, but she got the feeling that now was not the time. Not today...

'I only know one person who has ever found the centre. It was my friend's father who planted the hedges.'

Flora bit her lip and pondered. How difficult could an old labyrinth really be? But if Egon had tried several times without any luck...

'Well, maybe I'll give it a miss then.'

'Probably for the best. It's cold today. Much more pleasant to get lost on a warm and sunny day.'

Flora took a closer look at Egon. He was tall and thin and had a slightly stooped posture, as tall people often do. He was wearing a loose jacket over a thick knitted jumper and green trousers. Dark hair stuck out from under his green flat cap and his glasses were slightly crooked. He straightened them and gave Flora a friendly smile as he took something out of his pocket. A book.

'What sort of book is that?'

'This? It's called *The Mysterious Island.* It's fantastic.'

'I've read that too,' said Flora excitedly.

Dad had loved the author Jules Verne and borrowed all his books from the library for her. She didn't love them quite as much as her father had, but maybe she would give them another chance now that she was older and smarter.

'Is there a library nearby?' she asked.

'Naturally,' said Egon, waving his book. 'This is from the library.'

'Great.'

There was something about Egon that seemed vaguely familiar, though Flora was sure she had never met him before. It was strangely easy to talk to him, despite his old-fashioned style of speech. She didn't think she had ever spoken to an older boy before. In the city she tried to avoid talking to boys altogether. Most of them just said really nasty things. But Egon looked kind, with his crooked glasses and stoop.

'Do you live here in Helmersbruk?' she asked.

'Of course. Father, Mother, my brothers and I. Though it is only my little brother and I at home now. I am looking after him.'

'Where's your little brother then?'

'He's sleeping, so I took the opportunity to take a stroll and search for my spectacles. But I suppose he is due to wake up soon. It has been a pleasure meeting you, Miss Flora.'

Flora couldn't help but smile. It sounded funny hearing someone else call her Miss Flora, just like in her manor fantasies.

'Wait a minute, Egon, do you know where the greenhouse is?'

He flashed her a friendly smile.

'Do you mean the orangery? You need only walk straight in that direction, past those fir trees and the low stone wall over there.'

He pointed at the path and grove of trees that Flora was just about to head towards anyway.

'OK, thanks.'

When she turned around again, Egon was gone, just as suddenly as he had appeared. What a strange person he was. But Flora sort of liked his old-fashioned clothes and polite manners.

In fact, she felt rather exhilarated. So it wasn't only her, Mum and Fridolf living in the manor grounds. Egon's family lived there too somewhere. The grounds were large and she had only explored a fraction of them. Maybe she would find Egon's house another day.

She felt silly for not taking the chance to ask Egon more questions while he was there. Had he been inside the manor house, for example? And where was his house exactly? She suspected that Egon might be a bit more talkative than Fridolf.

Well, they were bound to bump into each other again at some point. Next time she would be ready to quiz him.

She came to the little wall Egon had pointed at, and when she walked past it, she finally saw the orangery. And now she understood why it was called an orangery, for this was no ordinary greenhouse.

Just like the manor, the orangery was dilapidated. Several panes of glass were cracked and the others were so dirty that

Flora could barely see through them. But the ornate cast-iron frame looked intact, though brown and rusty.

Long ago when the orangery was new it must have looked as though it was made of sugar crystals, thought Flora.

The question was whether it was a good idea to go in. What if an old pane of glass fell on her? Flora decided to take the risk.

The door was very stiff and she had to pull on it hard. Finally she managed to pry it open just enough to squeeze through if she sucked in her gut and held her breath.

She almost got stuck and had to yank herself free, lurching into the orangery with more force than intended.

And then she just stood there in awe.

Once again, she thought of the big greenhouses back home in town. The von Hiems orangery was more or less the same style, but smaller and much more beautiful. The building was small but the ceiling was high—so high that there was a little spiral staircase in the middle leading up to a balcony.

There was a moist and musty smell of soil, but a sweet perfume also wafted through the thick air.

Lily of the valley? No, it smelt of hyacinths, Flora realized. But she couldn't see any hyacinths anywhere. Everything looked dry and wilted.

She saw what she thought must have been palm trees too, except all that remained of them were bare trunks reaching all the way up to the glass ceiling. The floor was covered in dry leaves and debris, but Flora could also see a few large square stone slabs like a path between the overgrown plant beds. Flora stepped slowly between the slabs, which rocked under her weight but didn't cause her to lose her balance.

What must it have looked like when everything was in bloom? Maybe the residents of the manor sat in here on rainy summer days with sponge cake and a jug of lemonade, listening to the rain pattering against the windows and inhaling all the floral scents.

Sometimes Miss Flora hosts tea parties in the orangery. Her neighbour Egon comes to visit with his brothers. They talk and laugh and build dens out of palm leaves...

There was a rustling nearby and Flora caught a glimpse of something white and furry scuttling across the floor.

'Snow Squirrel, is that you? Is this where you live?'

But the white squirrel had disappeared again. Maybe it had already scampered out into the garden.

Flora looked around, past the spiky trunks of the palm trees and towards the back wall. Fridolf had said there should be some old tools still in here.

It was literally like traversing a jungle. An extremely withered and brown jungle, but still. Flora had to struggle her way past surprisingly sharp dried palm leaves.

Eventually she got to the brick wall at the back. And there in the corner she saw exactly what she had been looking for. A rake and a couple of spades stood propped up against the wall, all covered in cobwebs and dust. Various gardening tools hung from hooks on the wall as well. A little hand rake and trowel caught her eye.

Perfect. She stepped forward eagerly.

'Ouch!' she cried when a palm leaf scratched her left cheek.

Instinctively, she brought her hand to her cheek and when she looked down at her white mitten she saw a few drops of blood. Had she cut herself badly? Her cheek stung, but without a mirror it was hard to tell how big the wound was. A drop of blood fell on the floor of the orangery. Flora produced a handkerchief from her pocket and pressed it on to the wound.

Something rustled above her again. The squirrel, no doubt.

But then she heard them. The whispers!

'I am telling you, that's not her!'

'Of course it's her. But something else as well.'

'No, that's impossible.'

'She's trying to trick us. She's after the treasure. We have to get rid of her.'

This wasn't branches moving in the wind and making a sound like whispers. These were clear voices. The same voices as were in her dream.

But Flora was wide awake so this couldn't be a dream. The voices didn't scare her, because she had made up her mind that nothing in Helmersbruk was going to scare her. Instead they were making her angry.

'What are you doing?' she shouted up at the tops of the palm trees, where it sounded like the voices were coming from. 'Stop whispering about me!'

It made no difference whether they were ghosts, real people or figments of her imagination—they were being rude. Why were they spying on her? What did they even want?

'Now you listen here,' she continued angrily. 'My name is Flora Winter. You can stop wondering who I am, because that's my name, OK? Flora Winter. And you can keep your silly old treasure, I don't want it!'

The orangery went dead quiet. Flora listened intently as she peered up at the ceiling. But she couldn't see or hear anything.

Her cheek still stung but it didn't seem to be bleeding any more. Flora tucked her handkerchief into her pocket, walked over to the wall, and lifted the rake and spade down from their hooks.

'Fridolf said I could borrow these,' she said in a loud voice. 'I promise I'll bring them back when I'm done.'

It was still quiet. Flora began to work her way back towards the door.

When she was almost there, something came whistling through the air, so close to her head that she felt a breeze and cried out.

It was the white squirrel leaping down from the tops of the palm trees before slipping out through the crack in the door.

Then the voices spoke one last time:

'Let's wait and see. The girl will give us answers in time. Wait and see.'

HELMERSBRUK

Flora was so angry that she grumbled loudly to herself, startling some little birds into a flurry out of the hedge. She had promised herself, crossed her heart and hoped to die, not to let anything frighten her during her time in Helmersbruk, and she fully intended to stick to that. There was no way she was going to let a few whispering spies and a weird squirrel get to her.

She stomped defiantly back to the manor, sat down at the edge of the flower bed and carried on weeding. At first she worked frantically, but soon her anger wore off and she started to enjoy herself again. She liked sitting by the manor house as if it were her home.

Although the rake she had found in the orangery was old, it worked well. The metal prongs were a little rusty but the wooden handle was smooth and comfortable to hold. Somebody had engraved a fancy *R* on the handle. Maybe this rake used to belong to someone whose name began with R?

Just like the day before, she lost track of time while working and slipped into the world of her imagination.

I, Miss Flora, have a labyrinth in my garden. All my friends think it's terribly exciting, but no one has ever succeeded in finding the centre. Only I know the way. Only I know that in the centre of the labyrinth there is… there is…

No, that's where Flora's lively imagination ended. What could be at the centre of the maze? She would have to think about it.

After a while Flora heard footsteps, and eagerly turned around hoping to see Egon.

But it was Mum standing at the end of the avenue.

'So this is where you are, Flick. Good heavens, what a spooky old house!'

Mum looked up at the building with wide eyes and Flora immediately felt the need to defend it.

'It's not spooky. It's the most beautiful house in the world.'

'Well,' said Mum. 'It's undeniably handsome. I especially like the squirrel.'

Squirrel? Flora leapt to her feet and looked around, pleased that Mum had seen the strange little creature as well.

'Where is it?'

'Up there,' said Mum, pointing at the facade of the house.

Flora looked but the white squirrel was nowhere to be seen. Then she realized Mum was pointing at something else, something attached to the outside of the mansion.

It was some sort of picture on the wall, half hidden behind creepers. How could Flora not have noticed it before? She thought she had inspected the manor house thoroughly.

'What on earth is that?' Flora asked.

'It looks like a family crest.'

The painting very accurately depicted a white squirrel, as viewed from the side, in front of a large flower. Flora stood on tiptoe, as if that would help her see better, even though the family crest was hung several metres above.

'That's it! It's exactly the same.'

'Oh, sweetheart, what happened to your face?' Mum cried.

Flora had forgotten about the cut on her cheek.

'I cut myself on a palm tree,' she said.

'A what? A palm tree?' said Mum. 'Can I see? Well, it doesn't look too deep. But you should give your face a wash. And then I'd like you to come food shopping with me.'

Flora's stomach rumbled.

'Can we get something to eat right away in Helmersbruk?'

Mum laughed.

'I was going to suggest hot dogs at the kiosk by the bus station, but then you said you were tired of sausages.'

Flora's stomach rumbled again.

'Hot dogs,' she said longingly.

She quickly placed the rake and spade neatly beside the steps, then ran back to the Gatekeeper's Cottage to wash her face and hands.

Once they were ready, they set off.

They had a clear view of the sea today, but Flora didn't think it looked particularly nice. Just brown water that went on and on.

'I bet it's lovely here in the summer,' said Mum. 'Just like the Riviera.'

'Mm.'

'Strange that the town hasn't spread in this direction, isn't it? Nobody wants to live by the beach? But it being barren and untouched does make it beautiful, of course.'

Flora just murmured again, having caught sight of the creepy bridge they had walked over in the dark two days before. It looked old, like it might collapse at any moment. It was high above an angry watercourse that gushed out to sea.

'I don't like that bridge,' said Flora.

'Come on,' said Mum. 'It has railings, you're not going to fall.'

Flora crossed the bridge as fast as she could. There was something unnerving about the place. She didn't know why, but it felt oppressive and eerie. It was a shame that she would have to cross it every time she went into Helmersbruk.

The road between the manor and the centre of the small town felt significantly shorter in daylight. Soon they saw more houses and a church tower.

A few minutes later they came to the bus station where they had arrived a couple of days earlier.

But this time the town wasn't deserted, far from it. People were walking around, cars were driving by and an older lady in a little paper hat smiled at them from behind a hot-dog stand.

They ordered a hot dog and orange juice each and ate standing at the kiosk while they had a look around.

Helmersbruk actually seemed like a really nice town. Some of the houses were old and interesting, but there were a few boring modern high-rises as well, which looked totally out of place.

The church was probably the oldest building. It was built of big grey stones and had a black peaked roof and a belfry.

'There's a food shop, come on,' said Mum.

'Look, there's the library,' Flora shouted happily when she saw a library sign. 'I'd like to go there one day.'

Inside the shop, they each took a basket.

'Oh, by the way,' said Mum, 'I was at Fridolf's and asked if he needed anything from the shop. He asked us to buy tea, tinned tomato soup and crackers.'

'OK.'

They soon lost sight of each other as they began scanning the shelves. Flora was headed for the sweets section but happened to pass a rack of weekly magazines.

A headline caught her attention:

Amazing winter flowers—species that survive freezing temperatures.

She put the basket down and started flipping through the magazine. Maybe she could find out what kind of plants were growing in the flower beds at the manor. But none of the pictures resembled the little sprouts she had cleared space for.

'Why don't you buy the magazine and then you can read it in peace and quiet?' said the man at the till.

He was young and grumpy with a face full of pimples.

Flora glared at him as she put the magazine back.

Where had Mum gone? Flora looked for her while also putting a few things in her basket: crispbreads, macaroni and muesli. Good things to have in the cupboard in case Mum got so absorbed in her work that she forgot about cooking.

Finally, Flora found Mum at the fruit counter. She looked dazed.

'Well I never,' she said.

'What?'

'A local journalist just came up and started talking to me! She recognized me, can you believe it? She's read my books.'

'Wow. Cool. You're famous.'

'*And* she wants to interview me. I couldn't say no.'

'Why would you say no? It would be great to be featured in the paper.'

'Well, I don't know. I'll have to think about it. Are you ready?'

'I think so. I'm not sure we'd be able to carry any more than this anyway.'

Mum paid while Flora packed everything into four plastic bags. Then they started the walk back, carrying two bags each. They were heavy, so it was slow going.

When they walked past the church, Flora noticed lots of graves in the cemetery. Some of the headstones looked new, but she also saw a few rusty metal crosses that looked very old.

'Do you think this is where they are buried?' said Flora.

'Who?'

'The people who used to live in the manor. Maybe the gatekeeper and his wife as well. All of them.'

Mum shrugged, but it was only a tiny shrug what with the heavy shopping in her hands.

'Maybe.'

'Do you know who they were?'

'Not really. Just that the von Hiems family founded the factory that the town is named after. Helmer von Hiems was the man who owned the land, and "*bruk*" means mill or factory, so the town was called Helmersbruk. Some time in the eighteenth century.'

'Oh, really?' said Flora. 'What sort of factory?'

'A glassworks, I think. The ruins of the factory are still there. Didn't you see them by the river?'

Flora hadn't looked, she had been too busy getting over the bridge as fast as she could. She would have to take a better look on the way home.

'What happened to the factory? And the von Hiems family?'

Mum was getting out of breath.

'God, these bags weigh a tonne. I don't know what happened, you'll have to ask someone else. I can't say I'm all that interested in rich old families.'

'Why not?'

'How interesting do you think their lives were? Especially the girls. Marry rich, have a bunch of babies, die young, no will of your own, no opportunities to make your own choices...'

It was funny that Mum claimed not to find the subject interesting because she managed to talk about it all the way back to the Gatekeeper's Cottage. Flora inserted an 'uh-huh' or 'mm-hmm' every now and then but wasn't listening very closely.

When Flora opened the gate in the wall, the sun was setting behind the trees. The temperature had dropped, and just as they were about to go inside, a snowflake fell from the sky.

'Fridolf won't like that,' said Flora. 'He hates snow and ice.'

'Have you spoken to him?'

'Well, I tried the other day. He's not very talkative.'

'No, I noticed. I think we're the first visitors he's had in a long time.'

'Maybe he likes being left alone,' muttered Flora.

If that were the case, then she could relate. Knowing how to be happy in your own company was just good sense.

Mum unpacked the shopping and Flora lit a fire. It started up easily this time too. She seemed to have a special knack for it.

'Oh, look,' said Mum. 'Has our little guardian angel found a friend?'

She had noticed the porcelain shepherd on the bookshelf.

'Yeah, I found him up by the manor house yesterday.'

Mum picked up the shepherd and smiled.

'He's nice. Now you'll have to keep an eye out for the three wise men, Joseph, Mary and the baby Jesus too.'

'Huh?'

'Well, these must be part of a nativity scene, mustn't they? Have you seen one before?'

Flora shook her head.

'We had a nativity scene at my grandma's house when I was little,' said Mum. 'It was my job to display all the little figures on the dresser at the beginning of Advent. Except for the baby Jesus, who stayed in the box until Christmas Eve.'

'I didn't think you were into decorations,' said Flora.

'Maybe I was when I was little. I liked the three wise men best. They had such beautiful cloaks and crowns. Will you help me peel potatoes?'

They went into the kitchen and started cooking. Mum clicked on the radio, which was playing choral music. It was cosy in the yellow kitchen. Much more cheerful than life back home in the city had been for a long time.

Mum seemed happy, which made Flora happy.

'I met a boy up by the manor today,' she said.

'Did you? Was he nice?'

'Yes, and he'd lost his glasses, the ones I found yesterday. He lives here on the manor estate as well.'

Mum was about to grate a carrot, but instead she stopped and looked at Flora.

'Is that what he said? He must have been pulling your leg.'

'He was not! He lives here with his parents and brothers.'

'He probably meant that he lives in town somewhere.'

'No! He told me he was looking after his little brother who was napping. Why would he have left town and come all the way to the labyrinth if he was babysitting, huh?'

'Labyrinth?'

Flora groaned and the potato she was peeling slipped from her grasp.

'There's a labyrinth up by the house,' she explained. 'One of those hedge mazes.'

Flora almost regretted telling Mum about Egon. All she had done was ask a bunch of stupid questions.

'Well,' said Mum, 'I just thought we and Fridolf were the only ones here. But that's great that you made a friend. Was he cute?'

Flora groaned even louder and turned off the tap.

Suddenly a scream came from outside the house! Flora jumped and Mum turned very pale.

'What in the world?...' she exclaimed.

And the shouting continued.

'Help! Please help me!'

THE VELVET HAT

Fridolf was lying flat on the ground just outside the Washhouse. Mum got to him before Flora did.

'What happened?' she cried.

'I slipped,' Fridolf whimpered. 'Fetching firewood...'

'Is anything broken?'

'May—maybe.'

Fridolf was grimacing with pain and Flora was ashamed of having thought it was silly of him to worry so much about snow and slippery ground. Maybe he knew that the weather would become brutal as soon as the temperature dropped.

'Do you have a telephone inside?' asked Mum. She was trying to use her most reassuring voice, but Flora could tell that she was flustered.

'No... the nearest telephone... is in the restaurant down by the seafront...'

'Is it far?'

'Not too far. Just follow the coastline. Right out the gate...'

Mum looked at Flora.

'Will you be able to find it?'

'I think so!'

'Call the emergency services. Tell them to send an ambulance to 1, Passad Road. Hurry!'

Flora rushed off, past the Gatekeeper's Cottage, out the gate and towards the sea. It was already quite dark and there were no street lights. She could only hope that there weren't any potholes in the road or she might break a leg as well.

Was there really a restaurant down there? No one from town seemed particularly interested in the beach or the area around the manor. Flora hadn't seen anyone walking or driving by, at least. Well, except for that shady hooded figure standing outside the gate, of course.

But never mind that now, all that mattered was getting help for Fridolf. It was so awful to hear a grown-up scream in pain.

After Flora had been running for a few minutes, she did indeed catch sight of a building down on the beach. A low wooden building painted pale blue, with a large porch and ornate woodwork.

It certainly looked like a restaurant, but it was closed and boarded up. She could just about read a sign on the wall: *Sea Pavilion*. It looked like this restaurant hadn't been open in a long time. But next to the building was a phone booth with a light on inside.

This wasn't the first time Flora had called for an ambulance. She'd had to do it one night last year when Dad couldn't breathe and had to go to the emergency room.

She did the exact same thing now: took a deep breath as she dialled the number and then spoke calmly just like they had been taught in school:

'Hello, my name is Flora Winter. There's an old man who's had a fall and is badly hurt. We need an ambulance to number 1, Passad Road.'

The person on the other end said an ambulance was on its way.

Flora couldn't run back as fast as she had come because this time it was all uphill.

By the time she reached the outer wall of the manor estate, a car with blue lights on the roof was driving towards her along the dusky road.

Just then, Mum and Fridolf came out through the gate. Mum was practically carrying the little old man, who was still grimacing in pain.

'Mum! You're not supposed to move someone who might have broken something,' Flora said reproachfully. She had learned that at school too.

'I know,' Mum stammered, 'but Fridolf insisted. He would have crawled out by himself if I hadn't helped...'

Fridolf had stopped whimpering. Now he was grumbling in a very pitiful manner and muttering something under his breath.

'They won't be able to come in,' Flora thought she heard him say.

The ambulance came to a halt in front of them and two men dressed in white jumped out. Fridolf let them help him into the ambulance while Mum hurriedly explained what had happened.

'Are you coming with us?' asked the one of the paramedics.

'No, I don't think so,' said Mum. 'We're not relatives, just tenants.'

The man looked surprised.

'Tenants? In the haunted house? Now I've heard everything!'

The man hopped back into the ambulance and started driving in the direction of Helmersbruk.

'Poor Fridolf,' said Mum. 'He seems so frail somehow, even though he's not that old. How does he manage alone? I mean, what would have happened if we weren't here?'

'Why didn't you wait with him outside the Washhouse? They would have had a stretcher or a wheelchair in the ambulance.'

'Believe me, I tried. But Fridolf stubbornly insisted that the paramedics weren't allowed to enter the area.'

'Why?'

'I have no idea.'

'Weren't allowed? Says who? Him? Or someone else?'

'Please, Flora, I don't know. He might have been delirious from the pain. Come on, let's go inside.'

Flora wanted to continue discussing what Fridolf had said but stopped when she noticed something behind Mum.

Someone was standing in the darkness over by the iron gate, watching them. Someone tall in a duffel coat with the hood up.

For some reason Flora shivered. There was something ghostly about this person. She had felt it the first time too, but this time the feeling was even stronger.

'What is it?' Mum asked, turning to see what Flora was looking at.

But the hooded figure had backed into the shadows and disappeared.

The next day it poured with rain. Flora was woken up by the sound of raindrops beating down on the roof tiles. She stayed in bed for a good while before getting up.

Looks like today is going to be an indoor day, Flora thought. *At least until it clears up.*

But what would she do? School work wasn't appealing. And Mum probably wanted to be left in peace.

If only I had the key to the manor house, Flora thought. *Then I could run up the avenue with an umbrella and spend all day inside the most beautiful building in the world.*

Then a thought struck her. She could hardly believe it hadn't occurred to her before.

Surely the gatekeeper would have had the key!

Maybe he used to carry one of those weighty bunches of jingling keys on his belt, with one huge key that unlocked the gate in the wall and then several other smaller keys for the manor house, the Washhouse and all the other buildings.

Could the gatekeeper's keys still be in the cottage?

Flora could hardly contain her excitement at the thought.

If so, where were they? They were bound to be tucked away somewhere safe. In a key cabinet perhaps?

She started looking. The entrance hall seemed like a good place to start, but she found no keys there. Nor in the kitchen, despite looking through all the cupboards and drawers. She continued her search in the living room.

'Have you lost something?' asked Mum, sounding irritated.

'No, not really...'

There was no key cabinet downstairs. Flora went upstairs to her mother's bedroom. It was a little bigger than Flora's but the wallpaper wasn't as pretty.

Flora was taken aback when she saw a photograph of Dad on the bedside table. It was a nice photo; he was smiling with his whole face and his eyes were sparkling. The picture must have been taken before he got sick seeing as he looked so strong and sprightly.

Flora looked around the room. There wasn't much to it, just a small dressing table with a mirror and a few hooks on the wall where Mum had hung her clothes.

She went back to the stairwell and opened the door to the third room. It was empty, she knew. She had investigated it on the day they arrived, of course.

But what if she had missed something?

The air was cold and slightly musty. She turned on the overhead light.

The room was just as empty as she remembered, but looking around now she noticed a few more details. Like marks on the floor that showed where furniture had once been.

The bed must have been there. Something heavy over there, maybe a chest of drawers or a bookcase.

Did they have children too, the gatekeeper and his wife?

In one corner was a smaller door. Presumably a built-in wardrobe.

Flora opened the door and was greeted by a blast of freezing air.

It wasn't a wardrobe! Behind the door was a steep staircase leading up. Flora shivered, partially from the cold, but mostly with excitement.

The Gatekeeper's Cottage had an attic!

Flora had always wanted to go up into an old attic. They didn't have one at home in the city, just a basement storage room that wasn't exciting at all.

Had Mum noticed there was an attic? Unlikely. Would Mum be happy about Flora going up there? Also unlikely. But Mum only had herself to blame when she was this wrapped up in her writing.

Flora walked carefully up the stairs, which were old and creaked terribly. She hoped she didn't get splinters in her feet.

It was dark up in the attic, but Flora fumbled around with her hand and found a light switch.

A lone bulb dangling from a cord shone a small pool of light and Flora gasped.

What a place!

The attic seemed to continue for several metres in all directions from the stairs. It was hard to see what was there in the dark, but Flora could make out a broken rocking chair, a rolled-up rug, some sort of small stool, and a number of boxes and cases.

Flora walked over to the nearest pile of boxes.

Fragile—crystal was written on the top one. Sensibly, Flora took a step back. She didn't want to break anything.

She moved forward slowly in the semidarkness with her hands stretched out in front of her. She took tiny steps so as not to stumble.

Her fingertips slid over something wooden, then over cardboard, then empty space before her hand plunged straight through a thick layer of cobwebs. She recoiled in disgust.

Her eyes began to adjust to the gloom. She saw that the attic was mostly empty. The only items were gathered near the staircase and the little light bulb.

As she turned around to go back, she accidentally kicked something. Two boxes were by her feet. One was smaller and square, the other large and round. The small one was on top of the big one.

They look like an old shoebox and hat box, Flora guessed. *Could the shoes and hat still be inside?*

The boxes were light and Flora moved them over the floor to directly below the dim light bulb.

She opened the shoebox first, but there were no shoes inside, only a bunch of old letters and some strange junk... Flora picked up the top letter and unfolded it. *Greetings from Provence* was written on the paper, nothing more. But inside the letter was also a pressed flower that crumbled into pieces when she touched it, so Flora carefully put the letter back in the box. Best not to fiddle with the letters too much—they might all contain delicate pressed flowers.

A wide ribbon was tied in a bow around the hat box. Flora gently pulled the ribbon to untie the bow, then lifted the lid. There was a label on the underside.

B. Wallengren's Ladies' Outfitters Ltd. was printed on the label and something was written by hand underneath.

The handwriting was old-fashioned and the ink had smudged a little, but Flora managed to decipher what it said.

To my dearest Rigmor.

Rigmor. It was a strange name, but the more she thought about it, the more she liked it. Was Rigmor the gatekeeper's wife? Or daughter, perhaps?

At the top of the box was a layer of yellowed tissue paper, which Flora gently swept aside.

'Ooh...'

There was a hat in the box! And it was absolutely beautiful.

It was crimson velvet with a narrow brim. It must have been old but looked almost unworn. Flora held her breath as she lifted it out of the box and looked at it.

Did she dare try it on?

Her hands were shaking slightly as she lifted the hat above her head. Then she stopped herself. She couldn't very well sit here in the cold and dark while she tried on such a beautiful hat. She needed a mirror, at least.

Flora put the hat back in the box, switched off the light and walked carefully down the stairs with the box in her arms. She went into her room and, after a quick glance in the mirror, decided she should make herself a little more presentable before trying on the hat.

Her hair had been damp when she braided it that morning so now it was curly and almost pretty when she undid the braids. And rather than looking mousy, it had a slightly copper tone. It was probably just the light playing tricks on her.

She checked her reflection in the mirror and thought she looked quite pretty actually. Which was not something that occurred to her often. All the excitement and the cold in the attic had brought a little colour to her cheeks. She thought she looked a little more... grown up. What if she started a growth spurt and grew as quickly as the shoots in the flower bed by the manor?

She opened the hat box, lifted out the cold hat and put it on.

It wasn't too big or too small. It fit perfectly.

A sudden gust of wind caused the windowpanes to shake.

The lights flickered on and off down in the living room and Mum shouted:

'What on earth?'

Flora stared at her reflection, her eyes wide in alarm under the red hat brim.

A chorus of voices were carried on the wind, all urgently whispering the same thing:

'Rigmor! Rigmor!'

ROBBY, GONNY AND RIGGY

HELMERSBRUK, 9TH DECEMBER 1961

My dearest, apple of my eye.

At the time of writing, I am in Helmersbruk, having returned for the last time. The doctors say I don't have much time left now. I am not sorry, for I have had a good life. My body is still working but I realize that the time has come to commit my memories to paper, while I still can.

I was involved in a great tragedy that occurred on Christmas Eve of 1925. I have had to live with the burden of this guilt all my adult life.

I have come to terms with the fact that I will never know for certain what happened in those last hours before Christmas Day, because I was far from Helmersbruk at the time.

Perhaps an answer awaits me in the afterlife? Nevertheless, my story may prove useful, scandalous though it is.

My darling, please read this with love. Be merciful and forgiving, for those who follow their heart can sometimes end up on unfortunate paths. I am sure you have learnt this for yourself.

Now let me start from the beginning.

I don't remember the first time I saw Robert von Hiems. But of course, I know when the meeting must have taken place.

I was just twelve years old and deeply unhappy. I didn't want to go with my papa to a new country, a new house, a new life, but I had no choice. We had only each other, Papa and I, and he had trouble finding work in our home country.

We packed up our most important belongings. My teddy bear Morris, a few trinkets and photographs, and Papa's work tools. We sailed north.

I remember the director and his beautiful wife welcoming us to their manor. She leant forward to caress my cheek and said something to her husband which I didn't fully understand at the time, as I had not yet mastered the language.

One of the words I heard Madam use was 'robust'. She may not have known that we use the same word in my native tongue. It was hardly a compliment. What little girl wants to be described as robust? Although it was undeniably true in my case.

If Robert was around at the time, I didn't notice him. There were so many other new things to take in. Not that he would have noticed me anyway, being a few years older. He probably thought I was a baby.

Helmersbruk became my home and after a while I stopped feeling so unhappy. I went to school with the factory workers' children and made many friends.

The director's sons had a governess who taught them at home, and sometimes I played with them too. They were called Robby and Gonny, and consequently I was promptly nicknamed Riggy.

Robby, Gonny and Riggy. We had a lot of fun together.

I mostly hung around with Gonny, who was closer to me in age.

We both liked books about adventures and heroic deeds. But our favourite thing to do was tease Robby in various ways. He was always trying to act so grown up and superior, but as soon as we teased him he would forget himself, lose his temper and chase us through the manor grounds while we whooped and laughed.

A few years later Robby, or Robert, grew up and was sent away to live with relatives and learn everything he needed to know in order to take over the factory one day. I didn't miss him very much, because I had other playmates. Besides, I soon had something much more important to think about.

The director's wife bore another baby, their third son, and I was asked to be his nanny. It was an honour. Madam must have seen how responsible I was, taking care of Papa and our home and helping him with the gardening.

Of course I agreed to the position. He was so cute, the little baby, but I was terribly nervous at first. What if I dropped him on the floor? Or lost my grip of the pram on a downhill slope while walking in the grounds?

But thank goodness nothing of the sort came to pass. We got on well, the baby and I. I sang all the songs I knew to him and whenever he got very upset I let him borrow my teddy bear Morris, even though he had much nicer toys of his own. But Morris, with his button eye and raggedy fur, was his favourite anyway.

I got a lot of praise from Madam. She gave me presents too: fabric to sew new clothes, a bottle of French eau de cologne she no longer wanted, and other fine and precious things. I felt cherished and valued, at least until the day I overheard her talking to her husband in the parlour.

'Such a simple, robust and decent girl, so good at providing comfort and cheer,' Madam said contentedly. 'It is lucky that she has such a plain appearance, else she might suddenly find herself a fiancé and leave us!'

I was still 'robust', even at the age of sixteen. I was strong and consistent, reliable and conscientious, and Papa was very proud of me. I had so-called green fingers and was almost as good a gardener as him.

I was certainly aware that I was plain, but it had never bothered me. I didn't have a fiancé, and neither did I want one, so Madam needn't have worried in that respect.

But then, when Robert suddenly returned home to Helmersbruk, everything turned on its head.

It was most inconvenient. And absolutely wonderful.

It all began one day in early summer. I could feel someone watching me as I was crouching in a flower bed. The weather was warm, I am sure my face was ruddy and sweaty, and it felt very unpleasant to have somebody standing there and watching me without making their presence known.

I looked around angrily and there, in the shade of a willow tree, I saw him.

He had grown big and tall and so handsome that I almost lost my head, though I had never been the sort of girl to moon and swoon and make a fuss.

'Good day, Riggy,' he said, and I could feel myself getting warmer. For some reason it felt very significant that this man remembered my childhood nickname.

'Welcome home, Robby,' I managed to say but then I was forced to excuse myself because I was sure I was as red as an overripe rose hip.

Oh, how wretched everything felt that summer, or at least for the first month or two.

I tried to pretend that everything was normal. I helped Papa in the garden and performed my care duties for the baby. But I was on my guard the whole time.

Where was Robert? Would I catch a glimpse of him? And if he saw me, what would he think of my appearance? Then when he did appear, my cheeks reddened and my breath quickened.

In other words, I was behaving like a complete sap and was terribly ashamed of my silliness.

Of course, it was unthinkable that a soon-to-be factory director like Robert von Hiems would have eyes for the gardener's daughter. Surely such a dalliance could never lead anywhere.

My feelings were so profound that I didn't dare tell a soul. I think Gonny knew though. He must have noticed how foolishly I acted when Robert was around. But dear Gonny was so kind and never mentioned it. He just smiled and continued reading his books.

Gradually, surprising things began to happen. I could hardly believe it, but it seemed as though Robert was seeking me out more and more often!

He accompanied me when I walked around the grounds with the pram. He would appear while I was talking to Gonny and want to join our conversation.

On more than one occasion I became aware of someone watching me while I was working in the garden, only to spy Robert's face up in a window or down by his prized automobile.

Sometimes he raised his hand in greeting when I looked back at him, and sometimes he just smiled his crooked little smile, probably unaware that it threw me into quite a spin.

At first I cursed myself for being so conceited. Of course Robert was polite to me, because I was one of the staff, and good manners were only fitting for a future factory director. Maybe he was keeping an eye on me to make sure I was working diligently and not slacking off during the working day? That would have made perfect sense.

But we were meeting and talking more and more.

After a while it no longer felt like we were master and servant, but more like it used to when we were playmates and it didn't matter that he lived in the manor house and I lived in a cottage behind the stables.

Fortunately, over time I got so used to his presence that I stopped blushing and stammering whenever he appeared. But sure enough, my heart skipped a few beats every time I heard his voice.

'Hello, Riggy, may I accompany you?'

With a mixture of terror and euphoria in my heart, I realized what was about to happen.

When summer ended, Robert left again, and I thought it was probably just as well. I shed a few tears alone in bed on the night he left, but the very next morning I made up my mind to stop indulging in silly fantasies.

I would work hard and be the sensible, reliable girl I had always been.

My childish infatuation would probably pass, I thought.

But then the letters started coming.

Robert disguised his handwriting so that it wouldn't be recognizable from the address on the envelope. I told Papa the letters were from a girlfriend. It was the first time I had lied to Papa and it didn't feel good, but how would he react if he knew the director's eldest son was writing to me almost every week?

Not that the contents of the letters were in any way scandalous. Robert just wrote *Greetings from Kosta* or *I have come to Lancashire, and send my heartfelt regards* and friendly things like that.

But each letter contained a special something.

A pressed flower or plant. Sometimes a herb or pansy. In the letter from Lancashire it was a rose that still retained its beautiful fragrance.

Robert never included a return address, so I couldn't write back, but I kept all the letters and flowers in a shoebox under my bed.

Even though he never said so outright, I knew the letters meant he was thinking of me, wherever he was in the world.

Naturally, this made me think about Robert von Hiems from dawn to dusk.

When I raked the autumn leaves in the avenue, I thought of Robert.

When we planted tulip bulbs for winter, I thought of Robert.

When we cut off dry palm fronds and planted Christmas flowers in the orangery, I thought of Robert.

When the baby, who had grown into a chubby little thing nicknamed Freddy, learnt to scamper around on foot, I thought of Robert.

Of course, the worst was in bed at night, trying to get to sleep. I would dangle my hand over the edge of my bed to touch the box of letters.

It almost felt like I could touch Robert himself.

And sometimes I wrote him letters too, but never sent them.

Sometimes I wrote sensible things:

Dear Robert, you must stop writing to me. It is inappropriate, and the letters are making me vain and irrational. Stop at once. Kind regards, Riggy.

But sometimes I wrote the truth:

Dear Robert, do you know that every time I receive a letter from you I hear music in my mind and smell lilacs in the cold autumn night? I think about you every waking second. Your Rigmor.

But I threw all those letters on the fire as soon as I had signed them.

I was dreading Robert's return.

I was also yearning for it.

THE SNOW ROSES

In the days that followed, Flora got into a new routine. Every morning she ate her breakfast in front of the fireplace and then spent a few hours exploring the von Hiems estate.

If it was too windy and rainy, she stayed in the attic of the Gatekeeper's Cottage. She had set up a cosy little space with the rocking chair and stool directly beneath the light. It was very cold in the attic but if she dressed up warm, in the gatekeeper's special cardigan and Rigmor's velvet hat, she was fine.

In the attic she found a stack of strange old magazines and flipped through them. She found a whole box full of scraps of yarn and crochet hooks and, following a pattern from one of the magazines, succeeded in making a small pot-holder to give Mum as a Christmas present.

When the weather was better, she went for long walks and worked in the flower bed outside the manor house. The hours flew by and she was often surprised when her growling belly told her it was time to go back to the Gatekeeper's Cottage.

In the evenings, she did school work and helped her mother with the cooking, cleaning and laundry.

She would happily live like this all year round. Life felt safe but also exciting, and strangely familiar.

The only problem was that she hadn't found her way into the manor house yet. She had looked everywhere and never found a key. She had walked all the way around the outside of the manor several times and tried all the doors and windows. They were all locked.

But exploring the grounds was fun in itself. It was a bit like a treasure hunt where Flora kept finding unexpected things.

She carefully studied the statues in the rose garden. They all represented women. One played a harp, another read a scroll, and the third carried a pot. She named them Serafina, Adalmina and Sabina.

They are sea nymphs, three sisters born from the same shell. They waded ashore to this beach several thousands of years ago. Serafina played music, while Adalmina read to the others from her parchment and Sabina made rose-hip juice from wild roses. But then one day a jealous woodcutter turned the beautiful sisters into stone, and here they have stood ever since.

It turned out to be such a good story that she wrote it down in the back of a school notebook. She called it 'The Legend of the Stone Sisters'.

A little way into the woods, Flora found a beautiful little lake and a mossy stone bench. The children of the manor must have bathed here in summer. And maybe went ice skating when it froze over? In any case, it struck Flora as a remarkably good place to be alone with one's thoughts.

This is the spring of wisdom and bench of thoughtfulness. Anyone with troubles can sit on the bench and gaze into the spring. Soon the answers will flow.

Further into the woods, she came to a summerhouse on a small hill. It was the perfect place for a romantic rendezvous, if someone were into that sort of thing.

One day when the weather was really nice, Flora took a packed lunch to the summerhouse and had herself a little winter picnic. She brought extra food and juice just in case Egon showed up too. But he didn't.

She didn't see the white squirrel either, or hear those annoying whispering voices—thankfully.

Flora was growing braver every day. Almost as if she was genuinely beginning to believe that she was Miss Flora of the manor, the rightful owner who needed nobody's permission to explore. Besides, poor Fridolf was still in hospital, so there was no one to ask permission from anyway.

The estate was large. Flora had tried to follow the wall all the way around to see if there were more gates, but in several places the grounds were too overgrown to follow the wall and she had to go in another direction, and then she would always stumble upon something interesting and forget what she was doing.

That must be why she hadn't found Egon's house yet.

She loved her walks, but she had to admit that she got a little lonely at times. She often talked out loud to herself as she walked, but she would have preferred it if there were someone who could talk back.

Then one morning when Flora was tidying the flower bed, she heard a voice.

'It's really coming along.'

Egon was perched on the porch railing, dangling his long legs.

'Where have you been?' Flora exclaimed.

He smiled even though he looked tired.

'My little brother has been very unwell. I've been watching over him.'

'Oh dear.'

Flora thought it strange that an older brother would have to look after his sibling so much. Where were their parents, or any other adults?

'It looks like the snow roses will bloom in time for Christmas,' said Egon.

Flora looked down at the shoots and their little green buds. More were appearing all the time and some looked almost ready to bloom.

'Snow roses? Is that what they're called?'

'At least that's what the gardener called them. Or actually he said "*Schneerose*" but it means the same thing.'

'*Schneerose!* That sounds like a sneeze.'

Egon laughed.

'Yes, it does rather.'

'Is he feeling any better, your little brother?' Flora asked.

'He is on the mend, thank you. And how are your family, Miss Flora?'

'Well, it's just Mum and me. She's fine. My dad is dead.'

'Oh. I am sorry. Did he die in the war?'

Flora smiled at his joke. There hadn't been a war in these parts for a very long time.

'No, Dad got sick and then about a year ago he... you know...' A lump formed in her throat and her voice became a little choked. 'He was my best friend.'

Egon nodded sadly.

'It must be wonderful to be so close to your father.'

'Aren't you close with yours?'

'My father is... how do I put it? He is a man of principles. He has to be, in his position. My little brother and I get off easy; it's worse for my elder brother.'

'Why?'

'He is destined to take over from Father one day, so he has a lot to learn.'

'Is that what your brother wants?'

'He has no choice. And as luck would have it, he is very clever. Not like me. I would make a hopeless director, short-sighted and slouching as I am.'

'Director? You mean of a film?'

Now Egon laughed out loud.

'You are a funny one, Miss Flora. I mean the factory director, of course.'

Flora felt silly. She had no idea about film directors or factory directors. She stood up, brushed dirt from her knees and hoped she wasn't blushing.

'Hey, Egon... have you ever been inside the manor?' she asked to change the subject.

But the porch was empty.

Once again Egon had slipped away without a sound.

A little later, as Flora was walking back to the Gatekeeper's Cottage, she heard someone speaking. She recognized Mum's voice. It sounded like it was coming from the other side of the house. Flora went to see what was going on.

'Oh, thank goodness, here she comes now,' Mum said when she saw Flora.

Mum wasn't alone. On the other side of the gate stood a

woman who looked about the same age as Mum. She had short blonde hair and a blue scarf and looked friendly.

'Hello,' said the woman.

Mum, who appeared to have been struggling with the gate, stepped aside and looked pleadingly at Flora.

'Could you open the gate, please? I don't know what I'm doing wrong. It's like it's locked again.'

Flora shrugged and walked over to the gate.

'Very embarrassing to have a guest and not be able to let them in,' said Mum.

'Oh, don't worry about it,' said the woman outside. 'This gate is notorious for it.'

Flora opened the gate. There was no trick to it.

The woman with the scarf narrowed her eyes and took a step back to avoid being hit by the gate as it swung open.

'Bless my soul!' she said.

'Flora, how do you *do* that?' exclaimed Mum.

Flora shrugged again. The real question was why Mum insisted that she couldn't open it.

The woman stepped quickly through the gateway, as though afraid the gate would slam shut on her.

'Hello, Flora. My name is Ann-Britt and I'm interviewing your mother for the local newspaper.'

'Oh yes,' said Flora.

They went inside. Mum and Ann-Britt sat down in the kitchen while Flora went up to her room. She lay on the bed and tried to read *The Canterville Ghost*, but Mum and the journalist were talking and laughing so loudly downstairs that it was difficult to concentrate. Nevertheless, it was wonderful to hear Mum laughing again. It had been a long time.

Flora put the book down, stared up at the ceiling and pondered.

There was something special about the people in Helmersbruk. Flora was usually very wary of meeting new people, but here she didn't feel in the least bit shy. She had taken an immediate liking to Fridolf, even though he wasn't exactly easy to talk to. And Ann-Britt seemed very nice too.

Not to mention Egon. She had liked him from the moment she saw him. It was frustrating that he always seemed to be in such a hurry to leave. If there hadn't been such kindness in his eyes, she would have thought it rather impolite of him. But she was sure Egon didn't mean any offence. Maybe he had suddenly remembered there was something he needed to do and just went off and did it, forgetting he was in the middle of a conversation? Dad used to do that.

Maybe that was why Flora liked Egon so much. He reminded her of Dad in a number of ways. Tall, kind and a bookworm. And now that Egon's little brother was feeling better maybe it wouldn't be too long until they saw each other again.

She picked up her book and continued reading.

After about an hour her stomach began to growl very loudly. She didn't want to disturb Mum, but she couldn't exactly just lie there starving either. She decided to go downstairs.

In the kitchen it seemed like the interview was over. Ann-Britt was packing her things away in her handbag.

'What do you think of Helmersbruk, Flora?' she asked.

'I never want to leave,' said Flora without thinking.

It was true. Time was passing too quickly. The thought of going back to their little flat in the city, back to school and the horsey girls, made her sick.

'Flora is really in her element here,' said Mum. 'She's out all day and comes home with rosy cheeks and sunshine in her eyes.'

Flora rolled her eyes. Mum was making her sound silly. But Ann-Britt nodded.

'I hope you know how lucky you are, Flora,' she said. 'A lot of locals are very envious.'

'Why?'

'Because you have free access to the von Hiems estate! This gate has been locked for as long as I can remember. The more adventurous kids have tried to climb the wall, of course, but as far as I know, no one has succeeded.'

Was Ann-Britt joking? It didn't make sense. Why couldn't someone simply climb over the wall? Then Flora thought of Egon and his brothers. They lived on the property. Didn't Ann-Britt know about them? But before she could say anything, Ann-Britt continued:

'I have certainly fantasized about the manor, the labyrinth, the forest lake and the Italian summerhouse, but never seen them with my own eyes. Have you?'

'Yes.'

For some reason, it bothered Flora that Ann-Britt knew about all these things. They were Flora's secret places! She knew that was a silly thing to think, but she couldn't help it.

She walked over to the sink, poured water into a glass and took a few sips.

'Ann-Britt, you must know something about the people who used to live here, don't you?' said Mum. 'Flora is dying to know and I have no idea.'

'The von Hiems family? They were a fabulously wealthy old family who came to live here in the eighteenth century, when they acquired this land as a gift from the King of Sweden.'

'Why don't they live here any more?' asked Flora.

'It's a tragic tale,' said Ann-Britt. 'The last family to live here died in a car accident fifty years ago. On Christmas Eve as well, which makes it even sadder.'

'Gosh, how awful,' said Mum. 'They all died?'

'More or less. They drove off the factory bridge, the one you cross to go into town. The car crashed into the river and everyone died. Two of the children, the mother and the director himself.'

There was a loud crash as Flora's water glass fell to the floor and smashed.

'Flora!' Mum exclaimed.

But Flora could hardly hear her.

'The director?' she mumbled.

'Yes, the last factory director. Hjalmar von Hiems was his name.'

'Clean that up now!' Mum scolded. 'And be careful of the glass shards.'

Flora knelt down obediently and picked up the pieces of broken glass.

Strange that she had never heard the word 'director' in connection to a factory before, but today she had heard it twice in the space of a few hours.

Of course, this Hjalmar von Hiems that died in the car accident couldn't very well be the last factory director if that was the role Egon's older brother was preparing for. Maybe Ann-Britt didn't know that family. Flora stole a glance at her while she was mopping up the water.

'Thank you so much for the chat and the coffee,' said Ann-Britt and stood up.

She continued talking to Mum while she put on her outdoor clothes. She said she would send a photographer round to take Mum's picture, and she would like to invite her for a cup of coffee as a thank you for the interview. Or a glass of wine and a bite to eat, if she preferred. Mum said she would love to.

Suddenly Ann-Britt yelped: 'Ouch! What on earth?...'

Then she burst out laughing.

'Who's this crafty little fellow? He was taking a nap in my shoe!'

She held something up. It was a porcelain figurine. This one was wearing a crown and a purple robe.

'It's one of the three wise men,' Flora muttered.

Mum gasped.

'Really, Flora, apologize this instant! Enough of this nonsense.'

Flora clenched her jaw. She hadn't put the porcelain man in Ann-Britt's shoe, but she knew Mum wouldn't believe her.

'Sorry,' she mumbled and took the wise man from Ann-Britt's outstretched hand.

How had he ended up in Ann-Britt's shoe? Who had put him there? What did it mean?

For a moment she thought the porcelain man really did look rather crafty.

THE VON HIEMS MAGIC

Ann-Britt from the local newspaper thanked Mum for the coffee one more time before leaving the Gatekeeper's Cottage. She paused on the front step to gaze longingly in the direction of the manor.

'Hey, Flora... I don't suppose you would show me the manor? I've only ever seen it in pictures.'

'It's locked,' said Flora.

'Yes, of course, but I would love to see it from the outside.'

'She'd be happy to,' said Mum. 'Wouldn't you, Flick?'

Ann-Britt looked eager.

'It would be something of a dream come true! What do you say, Flora? Or are you very busy with your school work?'

Flora shook her head and put her outdoor clothes back on.

She didn't really want to share the manor with anyone. She felt like it belonged to her, even though she knew that was silly.

On the other hand, Ann-Britt seemed nice and Flora understood why she would be so keen to see the famous manor for the first time.

'OK, let's go,' she said.

They strolled off towards the avenue, Flora went and Ann-Britt followed a few steps behind. She looked all around and let out little expressions of appreciation like 'Ooh!' and 'It's even more beautiful than I imagined!' It almost felt like Flora was a tour guide and Ann-Britt a tourist.

'I bet you miss your friends back home in the city, right?' Ann-Britt asked.

Flora just shook her head. Ann-Britt didn't need to know that Flora didn't have any friends.

'How come you've never seen the von Hiems manor before?' she asked.

'Aha,' said Ann-Britt with a giggle. 'I suppose you've never heard about the von Hiems magic?'

'The what?'

'Now, I don't want to scare you, seeing as you live here and everything.'

'No,' said Flora hastily, 'I'm not scared. Tell me about the magic!'

'OK. There are actually very few people in Helmersbruk who have ever been inside the manor grounds. And you can be sure that many have tried. But it's just not possible.'

'Why not? You can just walk in.'

'You would think so. But usually that gate doesn't budge. I couldn't get it to open today either. Whereas you opened it easily, which I thought was pretty interesting.'

Flora scoffed.

'That's silly. Besides, the wall isn't that high. Couldn't someone just climb over it with a ladder or something?'

'No one has managed to do that either. I know several of my school friends tried when we were younger. They said afterwards that it felt like the wall got higher and higher the further they climbed. Even the strongest and most athletic gave up.'

Flora thought this sounded ridiculous.

'Uh... Mum and I got in. There was nothing to it.'

Ann-Britt stopped walking. She had a knowing look in her eye.

'But that's the magic, you see. The von Hiems manor *chooses* who it allows in.'

'How could an old house make choices?'

'I don't know. But it seems that you've been chosen, Flora.'

A shiver ran along Flora's spine. She was sceptical, but she would love it to be true. That she was special. That the manor had chosen to let her in but no one else.

'What about Fridolf?'

'Well, this is his home.'

Ann-Britt started walking again and this time Flora was the one lagging behind. Could it really be true? Fridolf and Egon lived on the property, so they could get in. But no one else. Except Mum and Flora, and now Ann-Britt because Flora had opened the gate...

Flora's thoughts turned to the tall, hooded figure that she had seen spying by the gate on two separate occasions. Was that someone who wanted to get in, but couldn't because the manor wouldn't let them?

'When Fridolf had a fall and the ambulance came,' said Flora, 'he wouldn't let the ambulance men come in through the gate to help him. Mum practically had to carry him out.'

'That makes sense. I'm not sure I believe in this magic personally, but I bet Fridolf does. He was probably convinced that the manor wouldn't let the paramedics in.'

'I see...'

'I was very surprised to hear that Fridolf let you rent the Gatekeeper's Cottage in the first place. No one else has ever stayed here before, you know.'

They had come halfway up the avenue and the front of the manor house came into view. Ann-Britt gasped.

'Oh my goodness! It's absolutely magnificent. Much more beautiful in reality than in the old photographs I've seen. What a gem!'

Flora felt a little proud for some reason.

They walked the last stretch slowly, almost as though they were sneaking in, until they came to the small courtyard in front of the steps.

'Good heavens,' said Ann-Britt.

'Mm. Just such a shame it's so run-down.'

'But that almost makes it even more beautiful. Wistfully beautiful.'

Flora agreed.

'Imagine being able to go in and look around,' she whispered.

'Yes, imagine,' Ann-Britt whispered back.

'If I lived here, I'd have my bedroom in the turret.'

'Yes, that would be wonderful. Did you know there was a library in there? I read about it in a book.'

Flora looked at Ann-Britt with wide eyes. A library in the tower! Just as she had imagined in her daydreams, with bookshelves from floor to ceiling. How incredible that her fantasy was a reality!

'But the house would need some serious restoration,' said Ann-Britt. 'Not to modernize it or anything, but just so it could stay standing, at least.'

'So why isn't anyone taking care of it?'

'Too expensive. Someone would have to find the von Hiems treasure first.'

Ann-Britt laughed when she saw Flora's face.

'That's the next part of the legend. Not only is there a magic spell, but long-lost treasure as well. Didn't you know?'

Flora gulped. Treasure. She had heard something about treasure. The whispering voices had mentioned it. Both in her dream and in the orangery...

'What kind of treasure?'

'The last factory director, the one who died in the car accident, you remember?...'

'Hjalmar von Hiems,' Flora recalled.

'Yes, him. He was a suspicious man, they say. He was very protective over the family wealth and hid it somewhere safe.'

'Couldn't he have put it in the bank or something?'

'He didn't trust banks either. No, he kept his riches in a secret place only his eldest son knew about. And his son was with him in the car accident. And now they're all gone: the father, the son and the treasure.'

Flora looked up thoughtfully at the house's flaking facade and broken windows.

'If I found the treasure, I would use it to restore the building,' she said.

'Yes, it deserves it.'

'What if the treasure is still here some—?'

Suddenly they heard a mighty crash and both spun around. Then another crash, and another. It was coming from the gate.

'It sounds like someone is trying to break in!' Ann-Britt said and began walking back down the avenue with brisk steps. Flora followed.

The noise was coming from a man banging on the large iron gate. He swore and cursed. And the gate roared and screeched back, as if putting up a fight.

'We'll break down this damn gate,' he shouted to someone sitting in a car behind him, 'if we bring a digger next time.'

When he noticed Flora and Ann-Britt, he looked embarrassed.

'Oh... I didn't think there was anybody here.'

'Right, and I suppose you thought you'd take advantage of this time while poor Fridolf is in hospital.' Ann-Britt sounded bitter. She seemed to know the man.

He took on an insolent expression.

'And you, star reporter, what are you doing here, may I ask? Who's the kid?'

Mum had come out of the house and stood next to Flora.

'The kid is my daughter. I'm Linn Winter and I'm renting the Gatekeeper's Cottage. And who might you be?'

The man said nothing, but Ann-Britt answered in his place.

'Linn Winter, meet Helmersbruk's mayor, Kjell Munther.'

Flora glared at Kjell Munther. Mayor sounded like a respectable title. Why was this mayor bashing on an old gate? What did he want?

Suddenly his face lit up.

'Oh, you're staying in the Gatekeeper's Cottage? Then you might have seen the key to the main gate. Big old thing, heavy.'

'No,' Flora and Mum said in unison.

Even if she did know where the key was, Flora wouldn't have given it to Kjell Munther. She hoped that the magic Ann-Britt had told her about was real. She really didn't want him to enter the manor estate. He looked like he had bad intentions.

Kjell Munther swore and let go of the gate.

'It's no use. The piece of junk won't budge.'

Then the car door opened. A high-heeled brown leather boot appeared. Then the other. Then the rest of the woman emerged, slowly and theatrically.

She had long blonde hair and very expensive-looking clothes, and was wearing sunglasses even though it wasn't sunny. The corners of her lips were drawn down in a sour, involuntary frown.

'Of course, I should have known,' Ann-Britt said with a sigh.

Flora looked at her questioningly and then back at the woman in the boots. Who was she?

The woman pretended not to see Mum, Flora and Ann-Britt.

'Is this the only way on to the property?' she said.

Her voice was high-pitched but a little hoarse and raspy at the same time.

'The only way to drive in, yes. A wall surrounds the entire estate,' said Kjell Munther.

'How did those three get in then?'

She nodded in the direction of Flora and the others without looking at them.

'There's a smaller gate over there.'

'Well, then.'

The woman began walking along the wall towards the small gate that led into the little garden of the Gatekeeper's Cottage.

'I'd think twice about doing that if I were you, Mrs Marton,' shouted Ann-Britt. 'What would people think if they read in the paper that Dagmar Marton and Kjell Munther tried to sneak into the von Hiems grounds when Fridolf was in hospital? It would look pretty suspicious, wouldn't it? Like you were trespassing.'

Dagmar Marton stopped but didn't turn around. She stood there for a moment, as though weighing it up. Then she walked slowly back to the car.

'We'll have to come back another day, Kjell,' she said.

'All right, all right. Fine,' said Kjell Munther.

When Dagmar Marton opened the car door, Flora saw that there was someone in the backseat as well, but she couldn't make them out. They looked like little more than a dark shadow. But for some reason Flora got goosebumps all over her body. Then she realized that the shadowy figure was looking straight at her.

'You know what, Kjell? I've just had a marvellous idea,' said Dagmar Marton, stopping outside the car. 'Why not invite the press next time we visit the property? Not the *local* press, of course, but the major national newspapers. Our hotel complex will be known all over the country from the very first day we open our doors. Just think what it would do for the town.'

Ann-Britt scoffed loudly, but Dagmar Marton continued:

'All the job opportunities, the tourism, the hospitality industry... they could write about Helmersbruk's bright future as a seaside resort. We can spread the news even while this derelict building is still standing.'

Then she pulled her booted legs back inside the car, slammed the door and drove away, sending gravel flying.

Suddenly Flora was freezing cold. Still standing? Hotel? What did the lady in boots mean?

'Ann-Britt? They... they don't mean... They don't want to demolish the manor?'

Ann-Britt looked sad.

'That's exactly what they want to do, I'm afraid.'

Mum gasped.

'But that's terrible! They can't do that, can they? Who was that blonde giant of a woman?'

'It's a long story,' said Ann-Britt. 'A family feud that goes back several generations.'

'Really? Tell me!' exclaimed Flora.

'The Martons and the von Hiems have been at loggerheads for hundreds of years. Some people in Helmersbruk even say that... well, it's pretty much slander...'

'What?' said Flora again.

'Well... you remember what I said about the von Hiems family and the car accident in 1925? Some claim that the Marton family had a part to play in it.'

'Huh? How?'

'Maybe they tampered with the car. But I don't believe it myself. The Martons are an odd breed, but they're not murderers.'

'Geez,' said Mum. 'This sounds like something straight out of a soap opera!'

'I agree. But now that the von Hiems family have almost died out, Dagmar Marton sees her chance. The Marton family have been waiting for two hundred years.'

'What do you mean that the von Hiems family have almost died out?' asked Flora.

Ann-Britt sighed.

'I mean Fridolf, of course. He never had a family of his own, so he has no heirs. And the poor guy is in bad shape, as you've seen. He can't take care of the property any more.'

'Fridolf?'

Flora couldn't figure out what that sombre little caretaker had to do with it.

'When his time runs out, that will be the end of the manor and everything else, sadly. Because he is the last in his lineage: Fridolf von Hiems.'

THE RING

That night Flora was woken up by a deafening din. It was coming from outside and just went on and on.

Her room was dark and she had no idea what time it was.

What was that terrible racket?

Once Flora had woken up a bit she recognized the sound. She had heard it on TV a few times and once in real life, the one and only time she had gone with Johanna to the stables.

It was the *clip-clop* of horseshoes! But why would there be horses clomping around outside in the middle of the night?

The floorboards were as cold as ice on the soles of her feet as she tiptoed over to the window, drew the lace curtain to one side, and peered out.

It was pitch-black and her breath formed a misty patch on the windowpane.

There were no horses to be seen anywhere.

Then the sound stopped.

'Did you hear the horses last night?' Flora asked when she came down to the kitchen.

Mum was drinking her morning coffee from a fancy coffee cup.

'What horses?'

'It sounded like there were several. Their hooves were really loud for a while and then the noise just stopped.'

Mum frowned and continued sipping her coffee.

'Sounds mysterious. I didn't hear anything. How are you feeling today? You were so sad yesterday.'

It was true. After Ann-Britt had left, Flora had run up to her room and cried for a long time.

She cried about the manor house being demolished and Fridolf, the last of an ancient lineage, being so frail and alone. She barely knew him, but still found it upsetting.

And once she started crying, the usual old things came bubbling up too.

That Dad was dead and was never coming back.

That soon they would have to go back to the city, the horsey girls and her uneventful, boring, lonely life.

That it was nearly Christmas but certainly wasn't going to be a merry one this year.

Mum tried to console her for a while but eventually gave up and said:

'OK, Flick, you just cry it out. It's good to do that sometimes.'

Mum was right. After a while the tears stopped and Flora fell asleep and slept soundly until those invisible horses woke her up.

'Are you still sad?' Mum asked.

'A little. But it's OK.'

Life didn't feel as dark and gloomy now that the morning sun was shining into the lemon-yellow kitchen. Besides, there was no point in wasting their precious time in Helmersbruk being sad. Flora would try to be happy today, despite everything.

She poured herself some coffee too and added lots of milk. It tasted bitter and not very nice, but it was comforting to sip something warm.

She padded into the living room, coffee mug in hand, and stopped at the bookshelf where the three porcelain figurines were displayed.

The angel from the pocket of the cardigan.

The shepherd she had found in the flower bed.

The wise man hiding in Ann-Britt's shoe.

It seemed as though someone had planted them for Flora to find. But who?

Flora's gut tingled as a thought struck her.

If the manor could choose who it let into its grounds... could it move objects too? Could it wind up music boxes?

The von Hiems magic.

Was the manor using these objects to try to convey a message to her?

Was there a reason why Flora could open the gate in the wall with ease while everyone else seemed to think it was impossible?

Could the secret be... the treasure?

The whispering voices that Flora had heard in her first days at Helmersbruk, in her dreams, in the avenue and orangery, had been silent lately. Flora was grateful for that. They were both creepy and annoying.

But the voices had said something about treasure. Flora closed her eyes and tried to remember.

'She's after the treasure!' they had hissed.

What if the von Hiems treasure wasn't a myth?

Maybe the treasure was still in the same place where Hjalmar von Hiems had hidden it long ago...

'What are your plans for today?' asked Mum.

'Thought I might look for the lost treasure of the von Hiems family,' said Flora.

'Mm. Sounds good,' said Mum, who wasn't listening.

She was already on her way to her writing corner. She would probably sit there until evening, eat dinner with a far-off look in her eyes, then continue writing until bedtime.

And perhaps that was just as well because it meant Flora could do her own thing without interruptions.

When Flora went outside, she stopped on the front step and gasped.

It had snowed! The grounds had been transformed into a magical winter landscape. It was so beautiful it almost hurt.

A wildness surged in Flora. Her legs started running as if of their own accord and the rest of her had no choice but to follow.

She ran across one of the large lawns. The grass was hidden under a blanket of snow that crunched delightfully under Flora's feet.

She ran with abandon like a toddler. Round and round, here and there, in circles and figures of eight. She had been running for a while and was out of breath but carried on for just a little longer, and then a little longer still.

Finally, she collapsed on to the snow, lay on her back and made a snow angel while giggling like a maniac at the heavy clouds high above.

She had never known snow could be this beautiful. She had never been into sledding or skiing. Her main experience of snow thus far was being pushed into snowdrifts at school. Once she had lost her bus pass when two of the horsey girls wrestled her down in the snow. Then Flora was scolded by the teacher when she came into class dripping wet. And the horsey girls got away with it. They always did.

Choosing to frolic in snow on her own was entirely different. She lay there for a while, panting and laughing while beautiful little snow crystals rained down on her from the treetops above.

When she finally scrambled up and brushed off the worst of the snow, she realized that her directionless dash had taken her to a part of the grounds she hadn't been to before. How funny, she thought she had been so systematic, but she must have missed this area. She was close to the perimeter wall, but in the distance she saw some buildings that she hadn't noticed before.

One looked a bit like the Gatekeeper's Cottage, but much smaller. It was completely dilapidated. The door had collapsed and the windows were broken. Still, the little house looked rather pretty, lined with shimmering snow.

Like a failed gingerbread house, Flora thought. She and Dad always made gingerbread houses that turned out as total failures. Either they were burnt in the oven or Dad would drop them on the floor after burning himself on hot icing sugar as they tried to piece the walls and roof together. But they always managed to save them by decorating with so much icing, sprinkles and sweets that the burnt gingerbread was barely noticeable.

'Modern architecture,' Dad would say. 'A stunning example of maximalism.'

Flora plodded a little closer to the 'gingerbread house' by the wall. Who could have lived there? Surely someone who worked at the manor. A chauffeur or gardener, maybe.

The other building was closer and didn't look habitable. At least not for a human. It might be a stable or something like that.

Flora's heart did a somersault.

A stable!

And what lives in stables?

Horses, of course! Horses with clattering hooves. Like the ones she heard last night.

But whose horses were they? Someone must have been taking care of them.

It wouldn't be Fridolf, who seemed almost incapable of taking care of himself.

Flora listened intently.

If there were horses in there, they were being very quiet. And wouldn't there be hoof prints in the snow and a musty smell in the air if there were animals nearby?

She walked closer to the building. The wind howled and a crow cawed in the distance. Otherwise, it was quiet.

She pressed carefully on the large wooden door. It opened immediately.

Flora's legs were slightly shaky as she stepped inside.

She had guessed right; it was definitely a stable. But it hadn't housed horses in a long time.

The stable was like a long corridor that ran parallel to the outer wall, with several small wooden pens on either side. Stalls, they were called. So she had picked up something from Johanna's horse chatter.

There was something mysterious about that clatter of hooves last night, Flora thought. It hadn't felt like a dream, but not quite like reality either.

What if... what if it wasn't real horses or a dream, but a message? A message to me. That I should come here to the stable. But what for? The stable is empty.

Or is it? Maybe there is something here...

The treasure. Imagine if this was where factory director Hjalmar von Hiems hid it!

Flora's heart started pounding even harder.

If the treasure really existed, she had to find it.

She would give it to Fridolf so that he could afford to save the manor.

That awful Dagmar Marton and slimy Kjell Munther would have to drive away in their fancy cars and never come back.

Then maybe Fridolf would invite Flora and Mum to stay in Helmersbruk and help him fix up the mansion, the grounds, the orangery and everything. He didn't have any family, so he would definitely need help.

She got so carried away with her grand plans that she almost forgot that she hadn't actually found any treasure yet.

But she was going to search for it. What did real treasure look like? She'd seen pirate treasure in comics and picture books—brown wooden chests filled with gold coins, sometimes with a royal crown and a few necklaces at the top. Did the von Hiems treasure look like a pirate chest?

She started walking slowly down the aisle, taking a good look in each of the stalls. She stopped and searched in each one, even though she didn't quite know what she was hoping to see.

Too bad the whispering voices were choosing to keep quiet now that she could actually do with some guidance. But maybe they would pipe up if they saw Flora get close to the treasure. They hadn't seemed to think she would be able to find it.

After Flora had examined the last of the four stalls without finding anything, she felt silly.

There was nothing here. No treasure chest, at least. But there was something about the stables, she was sure of that. The hooves had led her there for a reason.

Was there anything else she should be on the lookout for? A clue of some kind?

She went through all the stalls one more time just to be sure, but found nothing. No treasure, no clues. Could she have been mistaken after all?

So where should she search next?

Disappointed, Flora opened the door. The snow made it so bright outside that she had to stand there squinting for a few moments before she could see anything at all.

When she turned to push the stable door shut, something caught the light.

Sort of like when the sunlight reflected on Egon's glasses, Flora thought.

Wedged between two of the sturdy floorboards, something was glinting in the light. Flora knelt and had to practically press her cheek against the floor to see what was down there. It was something very small and golden.

The treasure!

Flora took off her hat and pulled out the hair clip she had in her fringe. Maybe she could pick the shiny thing out with the hair clip?

It was tricky but it worked. After some fiddling, Flora was left sitting on the floor with the object in her hand.

It was a ring. A gold ring with a small green gemstone. It must have been the gem that was glittering in the sun.

The ring looked old and valuable. Definitely something you would miss. Someone was probably looking for it.

And Flora had found it, just like that.

Was the ring part of the missing treasure? If so, where was the rest? Certainly not here in the stables, anyway. But Flora no longer felt disappointed. The ring was bound to lead her to the next clue.

Slowly she raised her eyes and looked up at one of the windows.

There on the window sill were a small porcelain donkey and ox. Flora could have sworn that they hadn't been there before.

THE LEGEND OF THE SQUIRREL

Flora had no intention of claiming the ring she had found as her own, but she decided to keep it on her anyway, so she could have it to hand.

Maybe Egon would recognize it. Or Fridolf, when he came back from hospital.

She wouldn't have felt right about wearing it on her finger. And leaving it loose in her pocket seemed like a bad idea. It could easily fall out.

Flora discovered a drawer full of ribbons and string in the kitchen of the Gatekeeper's Cottage and found the perfect thing: a black silk ribbon that might have come from a bow on a present once upon a time.

She threaded the ring on to the silk ribbon and tied it around her neck. It looked like a rather stylish necklace.

She put the porcelain donkey and ox on the shelf with the

others. There was a whole gang of them now. The angel, shepherd, wise man, ox and donkey.

'Are you going out again?' asked Mum as she fed a fresh sheet of paper into her typewriter.

'Yeah, I was thinking of going to the library.'

'Could you post a letter for me?'

'Sure. What is it?'

'Nothing exciting, just a letter to the bank. It's to do with Dad.'

'What about him?'

'After someone dies you have to deal with something called probate. And I thought I'd finished with all that, but apparently they're still missing some documents. So I have to request for them to be sent from the bank. Do you know where the post office is?'

'Yes, opposite the greengrocer's.'

Flora was looking forward to her visit to Helmersbruk library. Ever since Ann-Britt, the journalist, had mentioned reading about the von Hiems manor in a book, Flora had been desperate to find the book and read it. She hoped they would have it in the library.

Flora wanted to know everything there was to know about the von Hiems family, the manor, the grounds, and above all, the treasure.

She glanced at the avenue as she left the Gatekeeper's Cottage and her heart ached at the thought of the magnificent manor house reduced to a pile of bricks if that horrible Marton woman had her way.

There was nothing Flora could do to stop her either.

The only solution was to find the treasure. She touched the ring hanging around her neck. Finding it had felt like a promising start.

When she got to the factory bridge she slowed down. Now she knew why this place made her feel so uneasy.

It was somewhere here that the von Hiems family plunged into the rapids on Christmas Eve fifty years ago.

What did cars look like in those days? Were they those vintage cars that had to be started with a hand crank? They were bound to have been clunky and difficult to steer on a slippery road.

And Fridolf von Hiems, the youngest of the family, was at home in the manor. His entire family disappeared in a flash. No wonder he was such a serious person. You would never get over something like that.

Was that why he was so worried about snow and ice now? Because icy roads had cost him his entire family? Was that why he preferred living in the Washhouse to the mansion? Did the big building remind him of the terrible tragedies of his childhood?

Poor Fridolf. Flora knew what it was like to lose a family member. But at least she and Mum had had time to prepare for Dad's death. He was sick for a long time and so it wasn't a shock when it eventually happened. And they had each other, she and Mum.

Little Fridolf von Hiems had probably been sitting in the manor house eagerly awaiting the family's Christmas celebrations, and then his family just never came back.

It didn't bear thinking about. Flora picked up her pace and arrived in town ten minutes later. She went straight to the post office with Mum's letter and then on to the library.

Helmersbruk library was not particularly beautiful. It was one of those box-like buildings with big windows. But it smelt just like a library should: dust, coffee and the distinct scent of books.

Flora heard other visitors rustling, coughing and whispering among the shelves. It was a lovely, calm atmosphere.

Where might she find the book about the manor? Flora began to walk between the rows of shelves.

She found the children's section, but it was mainly filled with picture books. On the next shelf were lots of cookbooks. Where were the books about history and things like that? Maybe she should ask the librarian...

'Hello,' said a voice behind her.

Flora turned and froze. Three girls her own age stood there looking at her.

A knot formed in Flora's stomach. She was stuck in a dead end, between two bookshelves and with a wall behind her. The girls were blocking her escape route.

'What's your name?' said the girl in the middle. 'Are you new here? I haven't seen you before.'

Flora swallowed. The girls didn't look mean, but then neither did the horsey girls. They could act perfectly sweet when they were in the mood. Looks could be deceiving.

'My name is Flora,' she said. Her voice came out a little shrilly. 'I'm new. Or I mean... I'm only staying here for a little while.'

'My name is Petra,' said the girl in the middle.

'Matilda,' said the girl to the right.

'Anneli,' said the girl to the left.

'Hello...' said Flora.

'Nice to meet you.'

Matilda and Anneli went their separate ways, but Petra stayed behind. She looked at Flora as if she were the most interesting thing she had seen in a long time.

'Are you the one staying at the manor?' she whispered.

'Yes. Or no, Mum and I rent the Gatekeeper's Cottage. No one lives in the manor house.'

'Cool!' Petra exclaimed. 'Have you seen any ghosts?'

'No,' said Flora.

Whispering voices, invisible horses and knick-knacks that appeared out of nowhere, sure. But no ghosts.

Petra had fair hair, a sunny yellow sweater and a friendly face. But Flora thought it best to be on her guard. She was half expecting to see a wicked flash in her green eyes and hear cruel words coming out of her mouth at any second.

'We usually come here to do our homework,' explained Petra. 'Don't you go to school?'

'Well, back home I go to school, of course. Now I'm doing my assignments on my own.'

'What a shame you can't go to our school while you're here. There's only three girls in the class. It would be great to have another one.'

Petra smiled and Flora noticed that the corners of her own mouth were drawn upwards as well.

'Only three girls?'

'And seven boys. They're so immature, I can't stand it. Are you going to borrow a cookbook?'

'Um,' Flora uttered with a wary laugh. 'Actually, I wanted to read something about the history of the manor.'

Ugh, that sounded silly. But Petra nodded eagerly.

'Those books are over here. Come on!'

Flora followed Petra. She saw Matilda and Anneli at a table a little further away. They had spread out their textbooks, notebooks and pens all over the round table. They had apples and chocolate too. It looked like a cosy setup.

'Here!' said Petra, stopping at a shelf.

This seemed promising. The books looked old. Flora read the little labels on the shelves.

Art, literary history, anthropology, folklore, all sorts of big words. And then there was cultural history, architecture...

'What's that?' said Petra, pointing to the top shelf.

Flora looked up and gasped.

Up on the shelf, a small porcelain king was bowing to them.

'It's the second wise man!' Flora said softly and took the figurine down from the shelf.

How on earth had he got all the way to the library, so far beyond the walls of the manor estate?

She looked up at the shelf again. The wise man had been standing in front of a thick book with an emerald spine.

Written in gold letters was: *Helmersbruk: The Rise and Fall of a Glass Factory.*

The librarian refused to lend the book to Flora.

'You can't borrow a book without a library card, there's no way.'

'But, Hilde,' Petra piped up from the round table, 'can't I borrow it then? I have a card.'

Flora expected Hilde to tell Petra to be quiet in the library, but instead she answered just as loudly.

'No, you can't. You can only borrow books for yourself.'

'But I could always read it here in the library, couldn't I?' said Flora.

'Yes of course, but you'll have to come back tomorrow. We close at three today, which is ten minutes from now.'

Flora felt like roaring in frustration. She had barely had a chance to flick through the book and she was desperate to study all the photographs, drawings and descriptions that were hiding inside that green jacket.

Hilde glanced at her.

'Why so much interest in the history of the glassworks, then?'

'No reason,' muttered Flora.

Hilde nodded.

'I have an idea: I'll keep the book here so that no one else can borrow it. That way it will be waiting for you when you come back. How does that sound?'

It would have to do. Flora cast one last longing glance at the book, then put on her scarf and buttoned her jacket.

'Goodbye, Flora,' Petra, Anneli and Matilda all said in unison before leaving the library, chattering away happily.

'Bye.'

It was only when Flora was out on the street again that she realized she had pocketed the wise man. She had done it without thinking. It meant she had basically stolen something from the library, but there was nothing she could do about it now. Hilde had just locked the door behind her.

Besides, surely the wise man wanted to come home, to join his friends on the bookshelf...

'Hello, Flora! Have you been in the library?'

Flora was snapped out of her thoughts by the appearance of Ann-Britt.

'Yes, but they had to close.'

'I'm going to the city hall for a council meeting soon. I suspect that a certain mayor is going to make a passionate plea in favour of the plan to build a certain hotel...'

Ann-Britt looked bitter and Flora sighed.

That stupid hotel. If it weren't for Dagmar Marton's terrible plans, searching for the treasure would be nothing more than an exciting adventure.

'Come along to the town hall if you have time,' said Ann-Britt.

'To the council meeting?'

'No,' Ann-Britt said with a chuckle, 'but there is something I'd like to show you.'

'OK.'

The town hall was right next to the bus stop, so it wasn't far to walk.

'So, how's your mother?' Ann-Britt asked.

'Good. She's writing.'

'She's an incredible writer. Everyone should read her books.'

'Mm.'

Ann-Britt opened the door to the town hall and looked at her wristwatch.

'Ten minutes to the meeting, we've got time.'

They went up a flight of stairs and ended up in an oblong room with several doors. Flora looked around, confused. There was hardly anything there.

'Allow me to introduce,' Ann-Britt said solemnly, 'the founder of Helmersbruk, factory director Helmer von Hiems.'

Flora looked up at a portrait hanging on the wall. An old man in a white wig stared back at her. He looked haughty and rather bored. Apparently being a factory director wasn't much fun.

'So he was the one who founded the town?'

'That's right. Well, he founded the glass factory and had the manor built. The town grew up after that.'

'I see.'

The painting showed Helmer von Hiems next to a small table with a glass bottle on top.

And in the background were trees and hills, and something white...

Flora did a double take.

'Is that... a squirrel?'

'Yes,' Ann-Britt said with a laugh. 'A white squirrel. Do you know the story behind the von Hiems family coat of arms?'

Flora shook her head.

'It's said that when the family first came to this region, hundreds of years ago, a white squirrel lived in the forest right where the von Hiems family were going to build their house.'

'Oh?'

'At that time, people believed that white squirrels brought bad luck. They thought there was something demonic about their red eyes. But Helmer von Hiems claimed that this squirrel was his good-luck charm. And guess what?' Ann-Britt winked at Flora and continued in a deep, theatrical voice: 'Some say that the squirrel is still around today.'

'What? The same squirrel as hundreds of years ago?'

'Yes, according to the legend. There's always been a white squirrel on the von Hiems estate.' She looked at Flora and laughed. 'There are plenty of tall tales about the von Hiems family, as you can see. Magic, treasure, immortal squirrels...'

'Gosh...'

Flora had seen the white squirrel several times, but there was nothing out of the ordinary about that. Of course, she didn't believe it was several hundred years old. It was probably a descendant of Helmer von Hiems's original squirrel.

'Obviously it's just a story,' said Ann-Britt. 'No one but the von Hiems themselves has ever seen a trace of a white squirrel in the area.'

'Huh?' said Flora.

'I said no one but members of the von Hiems family has ever seen this white squirrel. They probably invented it to give their family crest an exciting mythology. Oops, I have to run! Say hello to your mother for me and thank her again for her hospitality.'

Ann-Britt disappeared down the stairs. Flora watched her for a moment and then looked back up at Helmer von Hiems's haughty face and the white squirrel behind him.

'This is all getting weirder by the day,' she muttered.

IT'S ALWAYS BEEN YOU AND ME

So, my darling. I took a break from writing for a bite to eat at a lovely little tearoom. It wasn't here during my time in Helmersbruk. And I don't recognize any faces either. I've forgotten everyone and they have forgotten me.

I made an attempt to visit the manor to bid a final farewell to the place I had once called home. But I couldn't bring myself to cross the factory bridge.

My legs refused to keep walking when I thought about the fact that this was where it happened. Where the three brothers whom I loved so dearly lost their lives in the rushing water beneath the bridge.

I had to turn around and go back.

Now I am sitting on a pew in the church and writing to you. The same sadness is present here too, but in a more peaceful way.

At the bridge there is nothing but horror and despair.

Anyway, back to my story.

Robert came home again when the first snow fell. I can picture him now, jumping out of the car and running towards the house with snowflakes in his hair and his scarf fluttering behind him.

He kissed his mother, shook hands with the director and jostled with Gonny for a while.

I was grateful to have Freddy in my arms. The little one was so rambunctious that I had my hands full and everyone probably thought it was the effort of holding him that was making me turn red in the face.

Robert turned his back to his parents and looked me straight in the eye while giving Freddy a little pat on the head. My knees almost gave out, but I held myself together.

The family sat down to dinner, except for Freddy, who was going to bed. After I had bathed him, fed him supper, sung him many a lullaby and put him to sleep, I went down to the kitchen to get my coat.

I found something under my coat. It was a hat box with my name on it! And in the box was the most beautiful red velvet hat I had ever seen!

I didn't dare try it on then and there, because Asta the cook or one of the maids might have seen me and wondered where I had got it from. Instead, I took the box with me and ran to our little house by the perimeter wall, and straight into my bedroom.

When I took the hat out of the box, a note fell out.

Meet me by the forest lake at midnight. It will be a moonlit night. Don't forget your ice skates! Your R.

That night, I sat on the edge of my bed for over an hour, straight-backed and fully clothed, except for my coat and shoes.

In case I heard Papa stir, I was ready to jump into bed, quick as lightning, pull the sheet up over my ears and pretend to be asleep. But I could hear his quiet snoring from the next room. He was sleeping soundly after a hard day of shovelling snow.

Poor Papa. It can't have been much fun working as a gardener in the middle of winter. If it weren't for the orangery with its palm trees and flamboyant winter flowers, he would probably have fallen into depression during those Nordic winters.

Finally, I heard the sound I had been waiting for: the big clock at the glassworks struck twelve. It was time!

I crept out of my bedroom and into the hall. It was difficult to lace my boots in the dark and I think I buttoned my coat up wrong, but it would have to do. Finally, after a moment's hesitation, I put on the soft red velvet hat, unsure whether he was expecting me to wear it or save it for a special occasion. Then again, this felt like a special occasion to me.

The manor was dark and silent in the winter night. Snow crunched under my feet as I ran in among the trees. The snow was deeper there and I had to slow down. Soon I caught sight of the lake ahead. A soft white December moon shone in the black sky and made the ice on the lake shine like silver.

I tripped on something, maybe a sneaky tree root under the snow, and almost lost my balance. I was about to fall straight into a snowdrift when I was caught by a pair of arms and heard the most beautiful voice in the world whispering:

'Please be careful! You can't skate with a broken foot!'

This wasn't our only nocturnal meeting that Christmas. There were several. Sometimes we skated on the lake, sometimes we met in the Italian summerhouse, and on one still and starry night we slipped down to the sea and took a walk on the ice outside the closed summer restaurant.

We walked, talked and laughed. Once, when I was in such a hurry that I forgot my gloves, he held my hands in his until they warmed up again.

It was all very innocent, much like when we used to play in the garden as children.

Yet there was a reason we didn't spend time together in daylight, though we never spoke of it.

The heir and the nanny. It wasn't appropriate.

What would the director and his wife say if they found out what was going on? I would probably be sent away. Papa might be fired too.

One evening Robert was late and I had to wait in the summerhouse for a long time. When he finally came, he looked so dejected, not at all like his usual self.

'What's the matter?' I asked, though I already had my suspicions.

It took a long time before he could bring himself to tell me what had been decided in the manor that evening.

And she arrived the very next day, driving up the avenue in a shiny crimson car.

Miss Wilhelmina Marton.

Her hair was daffodil-yellow, her coat was cornflower-blue, and her eyes were sorrel-green.

She looked like a real-life angel, albeit one with long slender legs instead of wings.

The wedding of Robert von Hiems and Wilhelmina Marton was supposed to take place that summer, but since Robert had not yet finished his studies abroad, it was decided to wait a little longer before the festivities.

Spring and summer were a real test for me, because Robert's beautiful fiancée visited her future home almost daily. Sometimes she came even when Robert wasn't around and just wandered the gardens by herself. Sometimes she spoke to Papa in a superior and condescending manner, as if she were already the lady of the house and he was her staff.

She was rude to Gonny and Freddy too, I thought. When Freddy got dirty in the garden, Miss Marton shouted that he wasn't to touch her clothes. She often declared loudly that Gonny was a bore who spent all his time in his library. I could tell that this upset him; he loved his books and I didn't see why he should be ashamed of that.

Mrs von Hiems, on the other hand, seemed to adore her future daughter-in-law. She was so elegant and refined—not at all 'robust'.

I hated feeling such contempt towards Wilhelmina Marton, but I was so profoundly jealous.

Robert would barely even look at me. He was rarely at home, and when he did come to visit his parents he hurried into the house, avoiding the nursery where I was with little Freddy.

I was terribly hurt that his feelings for me had cooled so quickly.

Freddy's love was my main comfort. Every day he would wrap his chubby arms around me and shout, 'Ringooo!'—which was the closest thing to my name he could pronounce.

Freddy often wanted to follow me and Papa into the garden, to use his little rake and help in so far as he could. It was very cute. Sometimes we let him chop wood, with Papa holding the axe as well, of course, to avoid accidents. And I taught Freddy my tricks for starting a fire quickly. You have to stack the wood in exactly the right way, and it will catch immediately. That sort of thing is good to know when you live in a big house with lots of fireplaces.

Freddy thought our simple home was a wonderful place. He wanted to examine all the photographs, especially those of my mother. He loved my teddy bear Morris, as well as the music box that we brought out for Christmas. He could listen to it for hours. I almost hurt my fingers winding it up, over and over again. He even claimed that my potato pancakes were his new favourite food, even though he had much fancier food at home in the manor house.

Yes, if it hadn't been for little Freddy, life would have been unbearable. Though my heart was broken, I struggled on.

Funnily enough, my heartbreak seemed to be an effective fertilizer for the flowers! Even Papa was surprised when everything I planted and tended to that summer bloomed well into the autumn. I spent my time digging, weeding, fertilizing, taking cuttings, watering and tending to my plants. I even planted some winter-blooming flowers, in case it turned out to be a mild winter.

The unhappier I was, the more lustrous my garden became.

Meanwhile, poor Papa was fully occupied with a huge, demanding project.

He was told to create a hedge maze.

The director had seen one at an English stately home and thought a replica would make a good wedding present for Robert and his future wife. He had no intention of waiting several years for hedges to grow tall enough for people to lose themselves in.

He paid dearly to ship in hedges that were already taller than a grown man. It was Papa's job to plant and prune them.

I wish Papa had spoken out against it. He was getting old and years of labour in various gardens had taken their toll on him physically. The labyrinth was far too much work for him, but he was too proud to say no.

I helped as much as I could, of course, but I didn't have a lot of time, what with looking after Freddy and taking on a lot of the gardener's usual chores while Papa struggled with this big project. He wouldn't let anyone else help, because it had to remain a secret until it was finished.

Soon I came to loathe the labyrinth as much as I loathed Wilhelmina Marton. Sometimes I fantasized about her getting lost in her own wedding gift and never coming out again.

I knew it was wrong to think such things, but a person who is so deeply unhappy can be forgiven the occasional spiteful thought, can't they?

One dark August night I was exhausted from a hard day's work but far too hot and dirty to go to bed. I took my bathing costume and walked down to the lake in the woods.

He was waiting for me by the bench. I didn't notice him until I was almost there. He fell to his knees in the moss in front of me.

'Rigmor, what am I going to do? I can't marry her, I just can't!'

It was the first time Robert and I had been alone since that winter evening in the summerhouse when he had told me he was engaged to Wilhelmina Marton.

I felt strangely furious with him.

I had really struggled all summer, averted my eyes when the young couple were out walking in the grounds, did everything I could not to break down. I hadn't shed a single tear, even though Robert had been ignoring me for months. And here he was, sobbing on his knees, a man destined to marry a beautiful girl, inherit a glass factory and live happily ever after.

'I think you can do it,' I said.

'Rigmor, she frightens me! She's as cold as ice.'

This calmed my anger a little because I understood what he meant. Wilhelmina Marton's cold gaze every day for the rest of his life was not an appealing prospect.

'A real man wouldn't be intimidated by a beautiful young woman. Now leave me alone so that I can swim.'

He slowly rose from the moss.

'Rigmor... have you really forgotten me so quickly?'

I didn't understand what he was talking about. He was the one who had forgotten me, not the other way around!

'All these years, Rigmor. Every time I see a flower I think of you, be it the smallest violet in a mountain pass or a magnificent rose in the grounds of a castle. I always think: these would thrive in one of Rigmor's flower beds. Just as I always thrive in her company.'

To my dismay, I realized that tears were welling up in my eyes. I wanted to appear unfazed.

'Rigmor... don't you feel the same? Have I got it wrong?'

'It doesn't matter what I feel,' I snapped. 'You know perfectly well that we can never be together. This has to end now! Leave me in peace, Robert!'

He was quiet for a moment. Then suddenly I felt him take my hand in his, with a light and gentle touch, as if he expected me to withdraw and didn't want to hold on against my will.

'But, Rigmor... it's always been you and me.'

I know I should have withdrawn my hand. But of course I didn't.

Now I have to take another break. I want to make sure I have time to visit Papa's grave before I catch my train.

The next part of my story is the most difficult. I must steel myself before I can write it down. Because it is important.

But unbearably painful to recall.

THE FOOTPRINTS

She ran across the snow, so light and quick that she didn't even break the crust. She arrived outside the manor house in a flash, jumped into the withered climbing rose and scrambled up, higher and higher.

Her expert, nimble paws found all the right places to grip the plant, and her bushy tail swept away the powdery snow, which rained down behind her. Soon she came to the window with a cracked pane where it was easy to squeeze in.

On she ran, across the floor, past the rocking horse and doll's house, past the small bed under its canopy, towards the rocking chair in the corner that was rocking rhythmically back and forth, back and forth...

Flora sat up in bed, out of breath and wondering for a few confused moments where her tail had gone.

It was hard to fall back to sleep after such a vivid dream.

Later that morning, Flora was humming to herself as she buttered her bread for breakfast. She had already lit a fire and heated a pot of water for coffee. Mum watched her in amusement.

'You've become so domestic, Flick. I hardly recognize you.'

Mum was right. Here in the Gatekeeper's Cottage, Flora really enjoyed preparing food, fetching firewood, washing dishes and bustling around. More than she ever did in their flat back home anyway.

'And you've been learning German too,' said Mum.

'German? What do you mean?'

'Why, your singing in German, of course. You've been singing German songs for a while now.'

'Oh stop, no I haven't!'

But Mum insisted.

'You sang a whole verse of that carol *Oh Christmas Tree*, except you were singing *O Tannenbaum*. I just sat and listened in admiration.'

'You must have heard wrong.'

'I did not! And one night when I got up to go to the toilet I heard you talking in your sleep, and that sounded like German too. Why didn't you tell me you'd started studying German at school? It's such fun. I've forgotten most of my German from school, maybe we can practise together?'

'I was talking in my sleep? What did I say?'

'I didn't catch everything. But something that sounded like *Schneerose*. Isn't that what we call Christmas roses?'

'Yes,' said Flora, relieved.

She actually knew the German word because Egon had taught it to her. Christmas roses, or snow roses, as Egon had called them. She must have been dreaming about the flowers and talking in her sleep.

'Shall I put the margarine back in the fridge?' Flora asked.

'You said something else too,' said Mum with a thoughtful frown. 'Oh, but what the heck was it again?'

'When?'

'That night. I went in to check on you and you said something quite loudly. It was almost a little frightening, you didn't sound like yourself at all. You sounded very determined. And very... well, German.'

'What did I say?'

'I don't remember.'

Flora rolled her eyes and put the margarine back in the fridge. Mum sounded like she had gone round the bend. She must have been spending so much time writing that she had started imagining things.

'I met Ann-Britt in Helmersbruk yesterday,' Flora said to change the subject. 'She says hello.'

Mum smiled.

'Really? How lovely.'

'You like her, don't you?'

Mum smiled even wider and nodded.

'It's rare to meet someone so easy to talk to. I can hardly remember the last time I made a new friend. It's not that easy for adults, you know.'

It wasn't that easy for children either. Flora had only ever had one proper friend. Johanna. And considering how quickly Johanna had changed, maybe she was never much of a friend to begin with.

Flora thought about Petra, the fair-haired girl she had met at the library. She had been easy to talk to. She thought they could be friends if only they got the chance to meet a few more times.

The same was true for Egon, even though he was a boy and a bit older than her. He already felt like a friend, even though Flora had only spoken to him a few times.

Maybe making friends was just easier in Helmersbruk than in the city.

'Too bad we have to go back home soon,' said Flora. 'Now that you've made a friend and everything.'

'Der ring gehört Wilhelmina aber sein Herz gehört mir,' said Mum.

'Huh?'

'That's what you said. In your sleep. "The ring belongs to Wilhelmina but his heart belongs to me." Is that from an old song or something? It sounds like the words to an operetta.'

Flora's hand involuntarily shot up to touch the ring she still had on the ribbon around her neck.

The ring. Was this the ring she had been talking about? She could have been dreaming about it and talked in her sleep.

But why in German?

And who was Wilhelmina?

'Are you absolutely sure that's what I said? The ring belongs to Wilhelmina?'

'Yes. Well, like I said, it was the middle of the night, so I wasn't entirely with it, but I'm pretty sure that's what you said. Wilhelmina.'

Flora had never known anyone by that name. She couldn't remember dreaming about a Wilhelmina either.

Was this like the horses' hooves? Did her dreams mean something? Was the name Wilhelmina a clue?

Flora ran out of the kitchen so quickly that she almost knocked over one of the chairs. What time was it? Was the library open?

She would run into town and read the book on Helmersbruk from cover to cover. Maybe this Wilhelmina was mentioned somewhere.

She quickly got dressed and rushed to the front door. It had snowed heavily during the night and the front step was so laden with snow that Flora had to struggle to open the door.

'You're not going out, are you?' Mum called.

'Yes, I'm going to the library.'

'I think you'll probably have to wait until they've ploughed.'

Flora was annoyed to admit that Mum was right. There was no way she could trudge through snow this deep all the way into town.

What a pain!

What if it took several hours for the snowplough to get there? Plus, it was Friday, so if she didn't make it to the library today, she would have to wait until Monday before she got another chance.

Stupid snow! Stupid bloody snow.

Since Flora was fully dressed, she decided to go out anyway. She would have to make do with a walk around the manor grounds instead–if she could even get there. She wondered how her flower beds had survived the snowfall.

She managed to push the door open and shut it behind her. Then off she plodded. It was difficult at first, but the snow wasn't as deep along the avenue because the crowns of the trees functioned as a sort of roof. There, Flora could walk almost as usual.

It was only a week until Christmas Eve, she realized. If Dad were alive and this were a normal Christmas, they would be decorating the house by now. They would display elves in the windows and light the lantern on the balcony in the evenings. They used to get the Christmas tree the day before Christmas Eve and leave it out on the balcony overnight.

Dad was always very particular about how the tree should look. The most important thing was that it be sturdy. Grandma's precious glass baubles, the ones that were still in their box back home, were heavier than those typical plastic ones sold everywhere. So they needed a Christmas tree with strong branches.

One year they went to five different Christmas tree vendors before Dad found one that met his standards. They had to carry it for quite a while, but they managed through teamwork. Dad held the trunk and Flora held the top.

Then, when darkness fell on Christmas Eve and the whole house smelt of mulled wine and meatballs, Dad took out the box of baubles and said what he always said:

'We'll hang these on the sturdiest branches, because they were Grandma's prized possessions.'

When she was halfway down the avenue, Flora could make out something pink in front of the manor house. It looked like flowers! But surely that was impossible. She walked as fast as she could.

It was flowers! The flower beds were so close to the house that the edge of the roof had protected them from the snow. And several snow roses, or Christmas roses or whatever they were called, had bloomed.

Flora clapped her hands over her mouth in utter delight. The brightly coloured flowers against the white snow and brown building were an achingly beautiful sight.

Was it thanks to Flora that the flowers looked like that? Or did they bloom every winter, whether someone cleared the flower beds or not? She didn't know, but she loved the idea that the flowers were alive and thriving because of her.

Miss Flora's green fingers, flower magic...

The flowers were hers. The manor was hers. She could pretend, at least.

She stared into the eye-window in the front door.

'Are you ever going to let me in?' she said. It came out sassier than intended.

Suddenly she felt like she wanted to teach the manor a lesson. As if it were a stubborn dear old relative who didn't mean any harm, but who could do with a bit of a talking to.

The manor didn't answer.

'If you want me to solve your riddle, find your treasure and save you from that horrible Dagmar Marton, don't you think you should cooperate?'

Flora marched up the stairs and grabbed the door handle.

'Well? What do you say?'

The door didn't budge. Not that Flora had expected it to, in all honesty, but she had hoped.

She still hadn't seen any sign of keys. Suppose they had disappeared forever? That's just what happened sometimes. Once Flora had lost her house keys and never found them again. Dad had to go to the shoe shop in the mall to have a new set made with a machine that made a horrible sound.

She sighed in frustration and, for the first time, felt almost annoyed at the manor. If the story about the magic spell was true and the manor really could choose who to let in through the gate, surely it could open the door for her easily enough as well.

But it didn't seem to want to. She only entered in her dreams.

She reluctantly went back down the steps. There was too much snow to go wandering around the grounds today. She would just have to go back to the Gatekeeper's Cottage and wait for the snowplough.

She stopped on the bottom step.

Strange.

She thought she had walked in a more or less straight line from the avenue across the courtyard to the stairs, perhaps with a slight detour to admire the snow roses, but there were footprints all over the place. They went here and there and didn't seem to lead anywhere in particular. She certainly hadn't walked around that much. And she hadn't seen any footprints when she arrived either. They must be fresh.

So someone must have been walking around while she had her back turned. But who?

'Egon?' she called.

It must have been him playing a joke on her. Where was he hiding?

She looked around eagerly and called out again. How could Egon run around so silently that she didn't hear him when she was facing the door? Even though she had noticed that he always moved very quietly.

Still, something didn't add up. It took her a moment to figure out what it was.

If Egon, or whoever it was, had made footprints in the snow, the trail would continue to where he was now. Maybe up to a tree or a hiding place behind a bush.

But the footprints were only in the middle of the courtyard. They didn't appear to begin or end anywhere.

And now that she thought about it... did they form some sort of pattern?

Flora went up the steps and climbed on to the porch rail. She stood carefully on the rail and looked back at the footprints, from higher up this time.

And now she could see. The footprints formed a word.

Knock!

Flora was so shocked that she almost lost her footing but managed to get down from the porch railing in one piece.

Knock? On what? She looked dubiously at the door.

On you?

Just below the eye-window was a knocker in the form of a brass ring.

Flora swallowed. Knock on the door. Was it really that simple?

She noticed her hand shaking slightly as she reached out, grabbed the ring, pulled it towards her, and let it fall back against a plate on the door.

Knock.

Knock.

Knock.

And the door to the von Hiems manor slowly opened.

THE NURSERY

After Flora had knocked and the manor door had swung open, she remained standing on the threshold with her hand raised as though frozen on the spot.

She stared into the silent darkness.

No one had opened the door. No one she could see anyway. It seemed to have swung open on its own.

The magic, Flora thought. *It's real. The manor chooses who can come in. And now it's chosen me.*

She had yearned for this ever since she first heard of the von Hiems manor. She had walked round and round, fantasizing about what might be inside, wishing with all her heart that the door would open to let her in.

And now it was happening.

'Right, I'll go in then,' said Flora, trying to sound casual, even though she felt like she had fizzy pop bubbling in her veins instead of blood.

She took a moment to stamp the worst of the snow off her shoes before stepping over the threshold.

Bang! The door slammed shut behind her. Flora jumped out of her skin. Was it the wind that had blown the door shut or was it the same unseen force that had opened it?

The first thing Flora noticed was a long staircase with black carved wooden banisters.

It was the exact staircase she had seen in her dreams! Except that in her dreams the wood had been polished to a high shine. In reality, it was covered in a thick layer of dust and cobwebs.

There were paintings on the walls but they were so dirty that she couldn't see what they depicted.

It was dark inside the house, but a little daylight filtered in through the murky windows.

Flora left footprints in the dust as she began to walk slowly around the ground floor of the mansion.

'It feels like I've been here before...' she murmured.

She wasn't sure whether she was speaking to herself or to the manor. But it felt necessary to break the compact silence.

When was the last time anyone had spoken in the von Hiems manor? When was the last time anyone had been inside at all?

She came to a large room to the left of the stairwell with an oblong dining table. Flora walked to one end of the table and stood behind the biggest, fanciest chair.

'The director's seat.'

Somehow, she knew it must be.

The table was set. Plates, cutlery and glasses in varying sizes were all laid out. There were twelve chairs around the table, but it was only set for five.

Apart from the fact that the glasses were full of dust and the crockery had turned completely grey, it looked like a family could sit down to a nice meal at any moment.

'Why didn't anyone tidy this away?'

On the other side of the stairwell was a study or office of some sort. A huge desk of dark wood stood in the middle of the room. There were also some bookshelves, a seating area, a fireplace and...

'Ugh, no!'

Flora recoiled when she saw the stuffed animal heads mounted on the walls. A deer and a boar stared down at her with blank, glassy eyes.

She decided to continue exploring upstairs. Flora could clearly recall what she had seen in one of her dreams.

Tall double doors. With light shining through the gaps.

Did those doors really exist? And if so, where did they lead?

She knew she had to be very careful walking up such old stairs. The wood might be rotten and she could fall through and be killed at any moment.

Flora made her way up slowly, but the stairs were solid—they didn't even creak.

And sure enough, there they were, right in front of her: tall double doors with a large brass doorknob. Just like in her dream.

Flora swallowed. She had goosebumps all over.

'I'm not afraid,' she mumbled. 'Nothing in Helmersbruk can scare me.'

She was close now; she could feel it in her whole body. So close. Was the answer to the manor's riddle in there? Was the treasure behind these doors? Could Hjalmar von Hiems have hidden it right there in the great hall?

'Here I am,' she said and noticed a slight tremble in her voice because she suddenly felt very solemn.

She put her hand on the doorknob and pushed.

Nothing happened.

No, of course! She had to knock. That was how it worked.

Flora knocked on the door. First gingerly with one knuckle. Then a little harder with the side of her fist.

And lastly, very hard and urgently with both palms.

'Well, open up then!' she cried out in disappointment and yanked on the doorknob. 'Let me in!'

But no. The door was locked.

There was a keyhole in the door. She bent down to peek inside. But on the other side was only darkness.

She heard a soft sound somewhere in the house. For a moment Flora thought it sounded like someone laughing. Maybe she should have been scared, but instead she just felt angry. Was the manor laughing at her?

'I only want to help! It's an emergency! Soon that Marton woman will come with a big digger, and then it will be too late!'

Silence. Tears started flowing down Flora's cheeks, but she stubbornly told herself that it was just from the dust. Crying out of disappointment was childish.

'Just wait. I'll get in one day!' she said resolutely to the double doors. 'Maybe not today, but soon...'

The idea of leaving Helmersbruk and the von Hiems manor and going back to the city without ever finding out what was inside... no, it was out of the question.

But she would have to let the double doors be for now. The mansion was big, there was plenty to explore.

She turned around and saw that the stairs continued to a second floor. What could be up there? Bedrooms, surely. And the turret! She simply had to look for the room in the turret!

Now she got excited again and ran up the stairs rather recklessly, but luckily these ones were stable too.

She found herself in a corridor with several doors and tried to figure out which one would lead her to the tower. It must be the one at the furthest end. There were no windows in the corridor, so it was almost completely dark.

If all these doors were locked too, she would be really disappointed.

Flora walked slowly, feeling her way with her feet so as not to trip. She kept her hands stretched out in front of her the whole time, and finally her fingertips met a wooden surface.

She felt around until she found a doorknob.

The door swung open silently and Flora realized she had been wrong. This wasn't the tower room.

It was a nursery.

She shivered. Not from the cold, but because she recognized this place.

She had seen this doll's house, this rocking chair and rocking horse. In that strange dream in which she had been a bushy-tailed little creature clambering up walls and slipping in through a broken window.

She had seen this little bed too. The four-poster bed with long hanging curtains in the middle of the room.

Flora didn't really want to go inside. She wanted to go and look for the turret, but something stopped her.

The dream of horses' hooves led me to the stables and to Wilhelmina's ring.

Did my squirrel dream want to lead me... here? Because I saw this room, as plain as day.

Why? What am I supposed to find in here?

She looked around.

The bed. There was something about that little bed...

She slowly crossed the floor with her gaze fixed on the long curtains. She accidentally knocked the rocking horse on the way and it started rocking back and forth. The runners drummed against the dirty floor.

Trrr-trrr-trrr-trrr...

Flora carefully pulled the curtain aside and dust showered down on the little bed.

There was something under the blanket.

Flora gulped, reached out her hand and pulled the blanket back.

All tucked in, on high-quality but dusty bedsheets, was an old yellow teddy bear.

Flora's hands were shaking slightly as she picked up the bear.

'Well, hello there...'

Whoever this bear had belonged to must have loved it very much. It had practically no fur left and one eye had been replaced with an ordinary shirt button. But the tattered old teddy looked friendly. Flora couldn't help but smile at it.

'Who are you? And who do you belong to?'

There was something else in the bed as well. A folded-up piece of paper.

She gently opened it and read:

To the best little Freddy in the world. Take care of Morris for me until we meet again. Your Ringo.

Freddy? Morris? Ringo?

Who on earth were they?

Morris might have been the teddy bear's name, Flora thought. It looked like a Morris.

But Freddy? She supposed it must have been the name of the child who had slept in this bed long ago. But Freddy wasn't a *real* name, it must have been a nickname...

'Of course!'

Now she understood. Freddy was Fridolf!

Could this have been Fridolf's room when he was little? It was strange to imagine that little old man as a child sleeping in this tiny bed, but it must have been his.

This was his nursery, untouched, while Freddy/Fridolf was all grown up and frail and chose to live in the Washhouse.

Had he just left everything behind when his family died on Christmas Eve all those years ago? Didn't he even want his toys?

Flora pressed the teddy bear's threadbare head to her cheek and walked over to the window, deep in thought.

Freddy was Fridolf, Morris was the teddy bear, but who was Ringo?

The only Ringo Flora knew was that guy from The Beatles, but she highly doubted this was anything to do with him.

Outside, the clouds had dispersed. The sunlight reflecting on the snow was so bright it hurt her eyes, but it was an incredibly beautiful sight.

Flora squinted at the treetops and snow-covered fields.

There was the labyrinth!

Curious, she leant closer to the window. She had been wondering how complicated the maze really was and wished she could take a look at it from above. And up here, from Fridolf's old nursery, she had a really good view, except for a few trees in the way.

The maze looked complicated. Flora tried to find the way to the middle with her eyes, a bit like when she used to try to solve the cartoon mazes in Mum's weekly magazines with a pencil.

But it didn't work. She just ended up feeling dizzy.

What she could see, however, was that the centre of the labyrinth opened out to a rather large space. Like a whole room without a roof.

What could be there? Maybe nothing at all. Or maybe something exciting! Would it even be possible to get through the maze now that it had snowed so much?

It was hard to tell from up there.

There was a rustling sound behind her and Flora turned back around to face the room.

There, on the armrest of the rocking chair, was the white squirrel! It was staring at her as if it had caught an intruder.

'Hello,' whispered Flora so as not to frighten it.

The squirrel didn't look easily startled. It looked at her resolutely with its little red eyes.

Then she heard something.

'What's she holding? She said she wouldn't touch anything!'

'It's just a toy.'

'Why was she let in?'

'Don't you recognize her? It's her! She's back.'

'How can we know that?'

'I don't like the look of her.'

'She's probably after the treasure.'

'Maybe she's in disguise. She's probably a Marton spy!'

'No, I am not!' Flora retorted.

Suddenly the squirrel moved, jumped down from the chair and disappeared out into the corridor.

'Wait!' Flora called and started running after it.

She only caught the briefest glimpse of whiteness far below her on the stairs. She would never catch up with the squirrel.

'Hey, you! Whoever is whispering and gossiping!' she shouted as she ran. 'Maybe you could actually tell me what I am supposed to do instead? Because I have no clue! And I want to help, do you hear me? I want to save the manor!'

Her voice echoed throughout the house. It was the only sound to be heard. The squirrel had disappeared and the voices had fallen silent.

Flora was back on the ground floor, just inside the eye-door.

The door opened again and cold fresh air poured in.

Flora understood that this was the manor's way of telling her it was time to leave.

'Yes, yes, all right.'

As she stood on the threshold, she turned around and shouted angrily:

'But I'll be back! You hear that, whisperers? Do you hear that, manor house?'

The door slammed shut behind her and Flora thought the eye-window was looking at her in amusement.

THE GRAVESTONE

'No, I'm afraid there's no green book here.'

Flora stared in dismay at the man sitting behind the front desk at the library looking completely uninterested.

'Could you please check again?' she said. 'That lady who was here before, Hilde, put a book aside for me.'

The man sighed deeply, as if he had been asked to do something extremely inconvenient. But he obliged and looked around behind the counter before shaking his head.

'Nope. What book was it?'

'It's called *Helmersbruk: The Rise and Fall of a Glass Factory.*'

He started leafing through a thick binder lying on the desk.

'Ah yes. Here it is. It's on loan.'

'Oh no!'

Flora felt numb. This couldn't be true! Someone had borrowed the book that she was so desperate to read.

The librarian gave her a funny look.

'They'll bring it back. You can borrow it in a month. That's how libraries work.'

'But I won't be here in a month!'

'Ah. Pity.'

A phone rang in the back room and the librarian shrugged before going to answer it. Flora was so disappointed that she wanted to jump up and down, reeling off all the bad words she could think of. She had stood right there with the book in her hands and not been able to read a single word of it—the injustice of it was boiling her blood.

Then her eyes fell upon the binder that the librarian had flipped through.

Who had borrowed the book? Maybe Flora could find them in the phone book and call to explain that she really needed it right now?

She leant over the counter and tried to read the page. It was tricky because everything was upside down. But eventually she found the right column and managed to read the name.

Borrower: Petra Marton.

An icy chill ran through Flora.

Petra.

Marton.

It took a while for the name to sink in.

It was Petra, the girl with the blonde hair and green eyes, who had borrowed the book even though she knew Flora needed it.

And what was worse: Petra was a Marton!

Could Petra be Dagmar Marton's daughter? They had the same fair hair. It was hard to know what Dagmar Marton looked like behind her sunglasses, but they looked similar enough to be mother and daughter.

Petra was on the enemy side.

The librarian returned. He seemed to have taken an interest in Flora all of a sudden.

'Are you the one staying at the manor?'

Flora just nodded.

'Cool! Have they started tearing it down yet?'

Flora hurried out of the library without answering. It felt like there was glue on the soles of her shoes.

When she emerged, a few jagged snowflakes fell in her eyes, making them sting and water. Then came the real tears and runny nose. She couldn't even bring herself to wipe her nose. She was Filthy Flora after all.

Everything felt hopeless. Horribly, hideously hopeless.

Flora had been so sure that she was chosen to solve the mystery of the manor. And maybe it was true, but what good was that now that her time in Helmersbruk was almost over?

The manor had chosen the wrong person for the task. Someone smarter, braver and more practical would probably have solved the riddle already. Would have found the treasure and saved the manor.

Someone else probably would have already figured out how to stop Dagmar Marton.

But not Filthy Flora. Freaky Flora. Failure Flora.

If only I had more time, Flora thought as she dragged her feet along the street. *Then maybe I could save the manor. But now it's too late...*

That Kjell Munther and Dagmar Marton had probably already planned it all. The diggers could arrive any second and start tearing down the house.

It was a terrible shame about the manor, but it was a shame for Flora too.

She was embarrassed that she had let herself dream about a life in Helmersbruk. She had imagined her and Mum being allowed to carry on living in the Gatekeeper's Cottage. She had pictured going into town to buy food once a week. Mum writing books and being best friends with Ann-Britt. Flora going to the local school.

Then she started crying even harder. How could she have been so silly and let herself be made a fool of like this again?

She had even daydreamt of becoming best friends with Petra and hanging out with Anneli and Matilda. She had thought they were different from the horsey girls. Well, the joke was on her. At least now she knew what Petra was really like.

She couldn't believe Petra had acted so friendly and helped Flora find her way around the library. She probably only did it to find out what Flora knew about the manor. And then she snatched the book right out from under Flora's nose.

No, Petra Marton was not like the horsey girls. She was even worse.

But the thought of going back to the city held no appeal either. There was nothing there for Flora. Nothing. Why couldn't Mum understand that?

Dad had understood. He always understood everything. Flora never had to explain things to him, he would just look at her, nod, and say or do exactly the right thing.

But Dad wasn't there. He couldn't help her.

Flora jogged along the outside of the cemetery wall. She was shivering with cold because she hadn't bothered to do up her jacket after leaving the library. What did it matter if she caught a chill and got sick? She would rather die than go back to the city, her old school and everything else.

Flora was so deep in her darkest thoughts that it took her a good while to notice a familiar sound.

It was that melody again. She hadn't heard it for a while.

Oh Christmas Tree. The music box.

The delicate tune rang out stubbornly on the wind.

The music was coming from the graveyard.

Flora stopped and couldn't help but groan. She was tired and sad and really not in the mood for solving mysteries right now. Anyway, what was the point? All she wanted to do was crawl under the covers in her bedroom with the floral wallpaper and have a good long cry.

But it was no use. She had to find out where the music was coming from. If she didn't do it now, she would wonder about it for the rest of her life.

The stone wall around the cemetery was quite high, but the snowploughs had left tall piles of snow beside it, making it easy to climb.

Flora listened carefully, trying to determine which direction the melody was coming from. It was hard. The sound echoed around the wall, the tombstones and the snow. For a moment she was sure it was coming from the right, then changed her mind and went left.

The cemetery was large and the paths between the headstones were covered in snow. Flora's legs grew tired as she plodded along.

Just then, the music box fell silent.

Typical. Had she struggled her way through this snow for nothing? Where would she go without the music to guide her?

She looked around helplessly. She found herself standing behind one of the largest tombstones in the entire cemetery.

What sort of people had such large tombstones?

Rich people, of course. Maybe the richest people in the community.

She made her way around the stone to read the text on the other side and, sure enough, it said *von Hiems* at the top in large, gilded letters.

For the first time during her stay in Helmersbruk, Flora felt a little shy. She had thought about these people so much, and suddenly there they were. All of them, just metres below her feet. What was left of them, anyway.

The headstone was almost two metres high and partially covered with snow.

Here lies factory founder von Hiems and his wife, Flora read at the top. Helmer von Hiems, the man in the portrait, the very first factory director.

A lot of people had been laid to rest in this grave. Most of their names had been worn away and were barely legible. The names became clearer the further down the stone they were carved.

Baltazar and Melvina.

Hjalmar and Jacobina.

Robert.

There was another name on the stone, but it was covered in snow, so she could only see the top edge of the letters.

Flora took a few steps forward and was just about to brush away the snow when someone cleared their throat behind her.

She spun around.

A tall, thin figure stood in front of her. It was wearing a duffel coat with the hood up.

Despite having sworn that nothing in Helmersbruk would frighten her, Flora was so terrified that she backed up and bumped into the tombstone.

This must be a ghost!

The ghost slowly raised a gloved hand towards Flora and pointed at her neck. Trembling with terror, Flora screwed her eyes shut. Could the ghost use its supernatural powers to strangle her?

'What are you doing with my engagement ring?'

Flora opened her eyes in astonishment. The voice certainly didn't sound ghostly.

It sounded like an elderly woman. A perfectly normal, harmless old woman.

The figure pulled down the hood.

'Oh!' Flora exclaimed.

For a moment, Flora thought it was Dagmar Marton standing in front of her. The thin face, fair hair and long legs were very similar. But this woman looked like an older version.

'Who are you?' asked Flora, now more curious than afraid.

The woman stood silently for a moment, examining her with her green eyes. The same green eyes as Petra, Flora realized.

'He was my fiancé,' said the woman, turning to look at the tombstone.

'Who was?'

'Robert von Hiems. We were due to be married in the summer. The von Hiems and Marton families were going to unite after a hundred years of feuds and rivalry.'

Flora looked at the stone.

Robert von Hiems 10.11.1901—24.12.1925

'What are you doing with my ring?' the woman said sternly.

Flora quickly untied the ribbon. This was the reason she had been carrying the ring around with her ever since she had found it in the stables: so that she could give it back to the owner if she met them. If the ring belonged to this old lady, of course she could have it back.

'Here. I didn't know it was yours. I found it in the stables at the manor.'

The old woman snatched the ring and inspected it for a long while. She took off her glove and looked like she was about to put the ring on her finger, then changed her mind.

'Damn you, Robert,' she muttered. 'You never should have done it, otherwise you might still be alive...'

'What did he do? Did he break off your engagement?'

It was clearly a very rude question, but Flora had no time for tact.

The woman looked at her. Her green eyes were cold but not unkind.

'He betrayed me,' she hissed. 'He betrayed me and brought shame on me and my whole family.'

'How?'

But the old woman didn't want to talk to Flora any more. She turned around and started walking towards the church. She had a poised and elegant walk as she moved through the snow, unlike Flora's clumsy plodding.

'Wait!' Flora called desperately after her. 'Are you Wilhelmina?'

The woman stopped, turned around slowly, and looked Flora up and down.

'I see,' she said. 'I thought there was something familiar about you. Now I understand.'

'Is your name Wilhelmina?' Flora repeated impatiently.

A strange, crooked little smile spread across the woman's face.

'It doesn't matter who I am. Soon I'll be dead and buried too. The more important question is: who are you?'

And with that, she walked away.

Flora found a rather grubby handkerchief in her pocket, dried her eyes and blew her nose. The feeling of total hopelessness she had felt before the music had lured her into the cemetery was easing up somewhat.

She turned back to the gravestone and tried to piece together everything she had just learnt.

Fifty years ago, the von Hiems and Marton families had apparently tried to put the past behind them and come together through the marriage of their son and daughter, respectively.

Now the daughter was an old lady in a duffel coat and the son was long dead.

But something must have gone wrong with that engagement all those years ago. A betrayal, the woman had said. So the rivalry between the two families continued.

How could the Marton family still hold a grudge after most of the von Hiems family had died in that car accident? To the extent that they still wanted to tear down the manor house and build a hotel instead?

Was it revenge they wanted?

It seemed utterly ridiculous when she thought about it. Why couldn't people just be decent towards each other?

There was a lot of snow on the von Hiems family grave and Flora wanted to tidy it up a bit. She carefully balanced along the edges because it didn't feel right to walk on somebody's grave.

First she swept away the powdery snow settled at the top of the stone, as far as she was able.

Then she carried on brushing the front. The names became clearer as she did so.

Baltazar, Melvina, Hjalmar, Jakobina, Robert and at the bottom, where the snow had obscured it, Egon...

Flora sank to her knees in the snow, too shocked to breathe.

There it was.

Plain as day.

Egon von Hiems 10.06.1908—24.12.1925

THE WRISTWATCH

That night, Flora had strange and frightening dreams. She was back at school, Petra had joined the horsey girls and they were chasing her. Mum was dead and Flora was standing by her grave with the typewriter in her arms and when she tried to speak strange, made-up words flowed out of her mouth and the typewriter started writing all by itself.

Egon, Egon, Egon, it wrote...

Flora woke up to the realization that she was sick. Mum couldn't find a thermometer but said that Flora was as hot as a toaster and had to stay in bed.

So Flora lay in bed all day, floating back and forth between feverish fantasies, dreams and reality until it was impossible to know which was which.

The wallpaper came to life; the flower stems grew, coiled and writhed.

Egon's name on the tombstone.

Egon with his green cap and brown spectacles.

Dead for many years.

Couldn't it be a different Egon lying in that grave? No, Flora knew it wasn't. There was only one Egon.

And he was dead. Yet somehow alive.

Maybe everything that had happened at the cemetery was just a dream? But then where was the ring? It wasn't around her neck any more.

'I don't have time to be sick!' Flora shouted when Mum was tucking her in. 'I haven't solved the mystery yet. I have to find the treasure...'

But Mum didn't understand what she was saying.

'You have to rest now, Flick. Don't worry. We'll be going home soon. Everything is going to be just fine.'

Flora lay in bed for several days. Luckily, she managed to sleep through most of it, but every time she came round she tried to get up and head out into the manor grounds. There was no time to lose!

But Mum was adamant that Flora was absolutely not allowed to go out until she was better. And when she tried to sneak out without Mum noticing, her legs were as wobbly as liquorice whips and she had no choice but to crawl back under the covers.

She wept bitterly in bed several times.

Why oh why do I have to be sick now?

Then finally the morning came when Flora woke up and felt better. The wallpaper had stopped moving. She felt her forehead, but it was hard to tell if it was warm or not. Her stomach was growling loudly, at least.

'Mum?' she called but got no answer.

She saw a note on the bedside table.

Flick! Didn't want to wake you. We're out of food, so I've had to pop out to the shop. Be back as soon as possible, Mum xxx

Flora scrambled out of bed. She still felt dizzy and had to move slowly. She staggered to the bathroom, washed her face and brushed her teeth.

Her nightgown was clammy and gross. She changed into a sweater and trousers, braided her hair as usual and immediately felt much better.

But her lips were as dry as sand. They really hurt.

Flora remembered having a jar of lip balm in her backpack. Was it still there?

She put her hand inside her red backpack and felt around. She found all sorts of rubbish: pencil shavings fallen out of a lidless sharpener, hard lumps of old tissues and a few paper clips. But no lip balm.

But wait, what was this? There was a hole in the lining of her backpack. Could the lip balm have fallen into the lining?

She reached in and felt around. Yes, there was something there, but it didn't feel like a smooth, round jar. What in the world could it be?

When she managed to pry the object out, she gasped.

It was Dad's wristwatch!

The one he had worn every day for as long as Flora could remember.

A fancy watch that showed the time and date.

The wristwatch she had worn at school when Dad died but put in her bag after the horsey girls had laughed at her.

Dad had taken such good care of his watch. Whereas Flora had totally forgotten about it and not even wondered where it had gone. There had been so much else to think about.

She put the watch to her ear. It was still ticking.

Flora made up her mind that she would never lose it again. She placed it carefully on the bedside table.

In the kitchen she found two broken pieces of crispbread and a tiny bit of margarine. She wolfed it all down and drank several glasses of water.

When she had finished eating she sat down at the kitchen table.

What day was it?

How many days did she have left in Helmersbruk?

She realized how much she wanted to see Egon. If he showed up now, she would force him to stick around long enough to answer all her questions.

Although... how do you force someone to stick around when they have been dead for fifty years?

She heard the sound of a car coming to a halt outside the kitchen window.

Did Mum have so much shopping to carry that she had taken a taxi back?

But then she heard a voice call out from the other side of the wall.

'Hello! Ladies in the Gatekeeper's Cottage! I need help.'

Flora quickly put on her shoes and jacket and ran outside. It was Fridolf! He was back from the hospital.

A taxi stood outside the gate. The driver had helped Fridolf out and would probably have been happy to accompany him all the way to the Washhouse, but Fridolf wouldn't let him.

'Thank you kindly, but she can help me the rest of the way,' he said to the driver.

Flora wasn't feeling all that strong after days in bed, but she had to help. Fridolf looked so frail. He leant on a cane and linked arms with Flora.

'Are you feeling better?' she asked politely as they passed through the gate.

'No, not really,' he muttered. 'And there's been snow too. Damn and blast...'

They walked slowly towards the Washhouse.

'I've been inside the manor house,' said Flora.

'Really?' said Fridolf. 'How did you get in?'

'I knocked.'

'I see.'

He didn't sound particularly surprised. Flora glanced at him as they continued walking.

'It's been a long time since anyone's been in there, hasn't it?'

'Oh yes. I had the house locked up on the twenty-sixth of December 1925.'

Flora stopped, which meant Fridolf had to stop too.

'You did? But you must have been tiny!'

'Six years old.'

'Fridolf... why don't you want to live in the manor?'

He muttered something inaudible in response, but Flora wasn't about to give up.

'Please, can't you explain? I want to understand!'

He glared at her, almost like a defiant child.

'I was too young to run the factory. So I was sent away.'

'Where?'

'To relatives. Distant ones, at that. Not very nice people. Didn't care much for children.'

'But what about when you grew up? Why didn't you want to move into the mansion then?'

He shook his head and tugged on her arm to show that he wanted to keep moving.

'Have you been inside the house since?' Flora persisted.

'No.'

'Why not?'

'Don't want to.'

'But the manor is...'

But now Fridolf was getting angry. He stopped and shouted:

'Are you deaf? I said don't want to! I can't! It was my fault, don't you understand? It's my fault they're gone!'

Flora was so taken aback by his anger that she was left speechless. If Fridolf had been taller, he would have frightened her. But looking into this little old man's sad face just made her feel sorry for him.

He was so lonely. Even lonelier than Flora. At least she had Mum.

He opened the door to the Washhouse and Flora helped him inside.

It was freezing cold inside the house. Fridolf sank down on a chair and let out a loud groan.

'I can make a fire,' said Flora.

She opened the damper, piled some logs into the stove and lit it. The room heated up quickly and Fridolf smiled weakly.

'You've always been so kind, so very kind,' he muttered and closed his eyes.

Flora peered into the small kitchen. In the pantry were cans of soup, peas, ham and all sorts.

It looked like Fridolf didn't go into town for supplies very often. He could have lived on canned food for several months.

'Are you hungry?' she asked gently. 'I can heat up some soup if you like.'

Fridolf didn't answer. All she heard was a gentle snore from the chair by the fireplace. He had fallen asleep.

Flora wasn't sure what to do. It was probably best to wait until Mum came back. Or maybe she was home already?

Flora ran back to the Gatekeeper's Cottage, but there was no one there. No one except Morris the teddy bear, who was propped up on the hallway table, his tatty old mouth showing a friendly smile.

Morris who had been bedridden in the nursery upstairs in the mansion for fifty years, waiting to come back to 'Freddy'.

Maybe now was the time? Flora took the bear to the Washhouse.

Fridolf was still asleep. Flora put more wood in the stove and had a look around.

The Washhouse was cosy, especially now with a fire crackling in the stove. Fridolf had very few belongings. A dining table, a few chairs, a bed, some potted plants on the window sill and stacks of newspapers and books. No photographs or ornaments anywhere.

Flora had never met her grandparents. They had all died before she was born. She glanced at Fridolf, who looked rather sweet dozing in his chair, and imagined that he was her grandfather.

She liked helping him. Who would take care of him when she and Mum went home again? Would he be all right on his own?

She put Morris in the middle of the table, leaning against an empty glass bottle with the note from Ringo in his lap. Fridolf would see it when he woke up.

Tea. She could make some tea. She had noticed some teabags in the pantry.

Flora sang to herself softly as she heated water on the stove and placed mugs, sugar cubes and teaspoons on a tray.

'O *Tannenbaum, o Tannenbaum*...' Flora sang.

'Ringo?' Fridolf said suddenly, startling Flora.

Had he seen the note and the teddy bear?

No, Fridolf's eyes were still closed. He was talking in his sleep.

'Ringo? Come back, Ringo...!'

'Er...' Flora said hesitantly.

Fridolf sounded anxious, as if he were having a nightmare. He grew more and more agitated.

'Gonny! He can't take Ringo, Gonny!'

'Fridolf? Wake up, Fridolf! I've made some tea.'

Fridolf opened his eyes and stared straight at her.

'Oh, thank goodness, there you are!'

Then he fell asleep again.

Flora waited impatiently at the gate for Mum. It was almost half an hour before she arrived, loaded up with several grocery bags in each hand.

'What are you doing out here in the cold? You've been sick!' Mum said reproachfully.

'Fridolf is back!'

Mum made some Bolognese and brought a portion over to Fridolf as soon as it was ready. He dutifully ate it up.

'That was delicious, thank you kindly,' he said.

Then they helped him to bed. He looked at them gratefully and fell asleep straight away.

'Poor fellow,' said Mum when they were back in the Gatekeeper's Cottage and sitting down to eat in the lemon-yellow kitchen.

'What do you mean?'

'He's all alone in the world.'

'Who will take care of him when we go home?'

'Exactly. He's probably too young to get a domestic carer, but maybe it can be arranged anyway?'

'But how would a carer get in?' said Flora.

Mum just laughed in bewilderment. She didn't know about the magic.

Should Flora tell her that the von Hiems manor didn't let just anyone through the gate? A domestic carer would be stranded outside if that was what the manor decided.

'We'll just have to hope for the best for Fridolf,' said Mum. 'I have to go back into Helmersbruk tomorrow. The post office was closed when I got there and I have to collect a package. A surprise for you, among other things.'

'Uh-huh. Great,' said Flora.

'Oh, and another thing,' Mum continued. 'I was thinking about inviting Ann-Britt to join us on Christmas Eve. She doesn't have family here, so she said she was planning on celebrating at the newsroom, which sounds rather gloomy. Would that be OK?'

'Then I'll invite Fridolf,' said Flora.

'Yes, that will be nice. Like a little farewell party before we go home.'

Flora's heart sank at the mention of going home.

'Do we have to?' she said softly.

'What?'

'Go home. Can't we just stay here?'

Mum looked at her, puzzled.

'No, of course we can't. We live in the city, Flick. And what about school?'

'There's a school in Helmersbruk too.'

'Yes, but you knew all along that we would only be here for a month. For a change of scenery. You weren't even that keen on coming, if you remember.'

'But I'm happy here.'

'Me too. It's lovely. Maybe we can rent another house here sometime?'

Flora stood up.

'I'm going to bed.'

'OK. Night.'

Dad's wristwatch was still on the bedside table. Flora put it on and held it up to her ear as she lay down.

There was something soothing about the ticking sound, even though the watch was wrong. The little date wheel said it was already Christmas Eve, and the hands read half-past six. They must be stuck. The second hand jerked back and forth as the watch ticked.

But that was a question for another day. Now she was as exhausted as Fridolf.

THE KEY

Flora felt deflated. The manor house didn't have the same allure any more. It would all be over soon anyway. The house would just be reduced to a pile of bricks and roof tiles, and the gardens would probably be dug up and destroyed too.

On the other hand, it was a sunny winter's day. It felt silly to just sit inside and stare into space when she had already been bedridden for several days.

Flora considered going over to Fridolf's to see if he needed help, but it was still quite early. He was probably sound asleep.

Flora felt like marching into the Washhouse and demanding that Fridolf tell her everything he knew about the treasure and Wilhelmina and the ring with the green stone and the white squirrel and the magic spell and... well, there was so much she wanted to know. But Fridolf would probably dodge her questions just like he had before. Or doze off in the middle of the conversation. Maybe he would be a little more alert after a good night's sleep? Flora would pop in to see him a little later, she decided.

Mum was already writing. Unlike Flora, she seemed unusually chirpy.

'Are you going out? I'm going to the post office in a bit, so I might not be here when you get back.'

'OK.'

Flora got dressed. She had no idea where to go and her feet felt heavy. But maybe a little walk would put her in a better mood. She hadn't been to the orangery for a while, for example. Or the labyrinth.

She started walking towards the avenue when she heard someone whistle and call her name.

'Flora! Over here. It's me.'

Petra Marton was standing at the gate and waving.

Flora's cheeks flushed hot.

Petra had some nerve coming to spy on the place. And to look so cheerful and innocent while she did so.

'Can you let me in? The gate is locked.'

Flora smiled grimly. There you had it. Flora had been fooled by Petra Marton, but the manor knew her true colours. The spell worked and Petra probably wouldn't be able to get into the property until her mother mowed down the gate with a steamroller.

'What do you want?'

'I came to give you this,' Petra said and pulled something out of her backpack. 'I waited for you in the library last Friday, but you never came. So I borrowed it for you.'

And there in her hand was *Helmersbruk: The Rise and Fall of a Glass Factory.*

Flora hesitated for a moment but then slowly walked closer to the gate. You had to be careful around people like her. Petra appeared happy and excited, but Flora knew it was just an act.

'I flicked through it a little. There's one picture you've simply got to see!'

Petra flipped through to the right page in the book and held it up. Curiosity got the better of Flora. She came closer.

'What is it?'

'Check out this picture. *The head gardener and his daughter,* it says. But, Flora, look. She could be your twin!'

Petra passed the book through the bars of the gate. Flora took it and glanced at the picture.

A serious-looking man in a peaked cap smiled awkwardly at the camera. In his hand he held a rake. It was just like the rake in the orangery, in fact it might have been the exact same one.

Next to the man stood a little girl. She wore a simple dress, knee socks and sensible shoes.

Petra was right, the girl in the picture really did look like Flora.

'For a second I thought it was you,' said Petra. 'But that's impossible, because the book was printed in 1962... Oh, what's this?'

Three cars in a row came driving along Passad Road and stopped just outside the gate. Flora recognized the car in front.

'Mum? What are you doing here?' Petra exclaimed when the tall blonde woman stepped out of the car.

Dagmar Marton, in the flesh.

'I might ask you the same thing,' Dagmar Marton replied to her daughter.

Flora hugged the book to her chest while she watched them.

Then Kjell Munther appeared with a smug grin on his face. Out of the third car came a tall, grey-haired gentleman in a brown overcoat. He was the only one of the three who took any notice of Flora on the other side of the gate.

'Good morning,' he said. 'My name is Agaton Brecht and I am a lawyer. Apologies for the intrusion.'

Flora didn't care what his name was, he wasn't coming in. And neither were the Martons or Kjell Munther. The manor would see to that.

Then she heard slow footsteps coming up behind her.

It was Fridolf. He walked slowly, supporting himself on a cane. He was holding an object in his other hand.

A large rusty key.

'No!' Flora gasped.

But Fridolf was already at the gate. He put the key in the lock and turned it.

The gate opened with a deafening screech, as if in protest.

'Oh, just let them in,' Fridolf muttered.

He sounded tired.

The gate opened wide enough for Kjell Munther, Dagmar Marton and Agaton Brecht to enter. Petra looked unsure at first, but then she slipped in too before the gate slammed shut.

All Flora could do was watch. How could Fridolf do this? Didn't he realize what he was doing? He was letting the enemy on to the property!

'Good morning, Fridolf,' said Agaton Brecht, the lawyer.

'Agaton. It's been a while,' said Kjell Munther.

'So you've really decided to go through with this? Perhaps we should talk in private first, just you and me?'

'Why?' said Kjell Munther. 'We have discussed the matter in detail, Mr von Hiems, Mrs Marton and myself.'

'When did this discussion take place?' asked Agaton Brecht. 'When Mr von Hiems was in hospital, I suppose?'

'Does it matter? Yes, it was at the hospital. Can't we go inside somewhere? I'm freezing my ears off out here. I have all the papers with me...'

Fridolf hobbled to the front of the small crowd of people and led them to the Washhouse.

Flora looked on helplessly as they went. Now she understood.

Fridolf had given up. He was going to sign Dagmar Marton's papers and give away the manor house, the grounds, everything. She supposed he didn't want the property any more. And he had no children to pass it down to either. He was the last of the von Hiems line. What did he care what happened to his childhood home after he was dead? He hadn't even been inside the house in fifty years.

Now all hope was lost. Tears burned in her eyes.

'Have you got any idea what they're talking about?' said Petra.

Flora had almost forgotten about her. Suddenly she felt furious with the blonde girl who was standing there playing dumb with those big green eyes.

'You can stop pretending now!'

'Why are you shouting at me?'

'Your mother's going to ruin everything! Build a hotel right here and demolish my manor!'

'*Your* manor?'

'Well, no, of course it's not mine. It's Fridolf's and he doesn't want it because he's sad that his family is dead. I seem to be the only one who cares about this place, and I can't stop them.'

'Flora, wait...'

But Flora didn't even want to look at Petra any more. Or at any Marton for that matter. They were vile human beings, the lot of them.

And Fridolf was a traitor.

She ran away clutching the book and kept running without a clue where she was going. She hurtled down the avenue, past the house and into the woods.

She didn't stop until she came to the lake and little stone bench. She collapsed on to the bench and screamed so loudly that her voice echoed on the frozen lake:

'Aaaaaaaaaarrrggghhh!'

Flora had failed. She had tried to figure out what the manor was trying to tell her, but she had been too slow and not smart enough.

How long before the Martons started demolishing the manor? They had been waiting for this moment for hundreds of years, they probably didn't want to waste any time. Flora guessed they would start as soon as the Christmas holidays were over.

Flora was still clutching the library book to her chest as though cuddling a stuffed animal for comfort.

She found a handkerchief in her pocket, wiped her tears and blew her nose. Then she just sat there for a while, gazing at the lake.

Then she opened the book and began flicking through.

The book was upside down, so the first thing she saw was the last picture in the book. When she turned the book around, she couldn't help but smile, even in the midst of her misery.

'Ah!'

There they were. The gatekeeper and his wife.

They stood on the steps of the Gatekeeper's Cottage with their arms around each other. He was tall and thin, with a bushy moustache and whimsical eyes. His wife was short and round and had dimples. Funny—they looked just like Flora had imagined! She read the caption:

> *Gatekeeper Eugen Gustafsson and his wife Margit lived in the Gatekeeper's Cottage until Eugen's death in 1955. They were the last of the servants ever to live on the property.*

She turned the page. The text was so small and dense that she decided to just look at the pictures. There were a lot of photographs from the glassworks and all the factory buildings that were mainly just ruins now.

At the beginning of the book there were painted portraits of the older members of the von Hiems family, including Helmer. She recognized him from the portrait in the town hall.

Was there anything in the book about the lost treasure? Or the legend of the white squirrel? There was no index or table of contents.

She stopped at another photograph and let out a deep, sad sigh.

A photograph from 1920. There was the last factory director Hjalmar von Hiems, standing with his wife Jacobina by his side. Their eldest son Robert looked about twenty years old. He was handsome and smiled at the camera. Next to him stood Egon, who must have been about Flora's age in the picture. And Fridolf was a chubby little baby, dressed in some sort of lace frock and matching hat.

It was so sad to see them smiling, unaware of the impending tragedy. The last of their lineage, the chubby baby, was now a frail, ageing man, and the house, in front of which the family posed so proudly, would soon be demolished.

Flora heard footsteps behind her and jumped.

'Egon?'

But it wasn't Egon. It was that tall lawyer.

'I hope I'm not disturbing you,' he said.

'How did you know I was here?'

He smiled kindly.

'It's hard to hide in snowy weather.'

Flora felt silly. Of course, he only had to follow her footprints in the snow.

Agaton Brecht sat down on the bench. He took off his hat and placed it between himself and Flora.

'Has Fridolf signed the papers yet?' Flora asked.

'No. As his lawyer, I have advised him to wait.'

So Agaton Brecht was Fridolf's lawyer, not Dagmar Marton's. Flora hadn't realized that, and it immediately made her like him a little more.

'My name is Flora Winter,' she said.

'Pleased to meet you. Call me Agaton.'

'OK.'

They sat for a while and looked out over the forest lake.

'There was something I wanted to ask your mother,' said Agaton, 'but I don't think she heard when I knocked.'

'She's gone to the post office,' said Flora. 'What were you going to ask?'

'I'm curious as to how you came to rent this place, you and your mother?'

Flora thought about it.

'Well... Mum wanted a change of scenery. I don't know why we came to Helmersbruk specifically.'

'It is something of a mystery. You see, Fridolf couldn't explain how it happened either.'

Flora looked thoughtfully at Agaton. It was all a little strange, now that he mentioned it. Why had reclusive old Fridolf suddenly decided to rent out the Gatekeeper's Cottage after all those years? And to two complete strangers?

'I can ask Mum,' she said.

'Please do, and kindly let me know when you've solved this mystery.'

Agaton stood up and smiled.

'It's a funny coincidence.'

'What is?'

'Your surname, Winter. You know what "Hiems" means, don't you?'

'No. What?'

'It is the Latin word for winter. So von Hiems and Winter are more or less the same name.'

Agaton Brecht said goodbye and soon the creaking sound of his footsteps in the snow faded into the distance.

Flora sat and pondered.

Winter and von Hiems. Winter and winter. She hadn't known that.

Winter was Dad's name. Mum's maiden name was Ljungberg.

Did this mean something? Or was it just a coincidence, as Agaton said?

When Flora got up to leave, she saw that Agaton Brecht had forgotten his hat on the bench.

When she picked it up, she noticed something underneath.

A small porcelain man with a gold crown and long, billowing purple cloak.

The third wise man.

HER MOST PRIZED POSSESSIONS

Mum wasn't back from the post office yet. Flora walked over to the bookshelf and placed the third wise man next to the other porcelain figurines.

She stood for a moment to admire the nativity scene, which was now almost complete. All that was missing was Joseph, Mary and the baby Jesus. The main characters.

'The last three had better hurry if they're going to be here in time for Christmas,' Flora said to the figurines on the shelf. She thought they agreed.

She settled into the armchair and opened *Helmersbruk: The Rise and Fall of a Glass Factory*. She flicked through to the picture of the gatekeeper and his wife. She looked at the photograph, then the room she was in, and back again.

It was easy to imagine Eugen and Margit in there. She was reminded of something that Fridolf had said: the residents of the

Gatekeeper's Cottage were such good people that their goodness had seeped into the walls and was still there.

It was plain to see from the photograph of Eugen and Margit that they were good people.

The door opened and Mum called:

'Flick? Are you in? Come and help me!'

Mum was carrying a large package up the stairs. Her cheeks were red and she looked happy and excited about something.

'Lucky the main gate was open, so I didn't have to call for you to get in, for once!'

Flora wasn't sure she agreed. Lucky that Mum could get in, sure, but that meant that anyone could get in. Even enemies.

'Help me with this, would you?' gasped Mum.

The package wasn't very heavy, but it was unwieldy and difficult to hold. *Fragile* was written across it in several places with marker pen, as well as *Linn and Flora Winter, 1 Passad Road, Helmersbruk.*

'Good job I took the sledge that was next to the woodpile,' said Mum. 'Otherwise, I never would have been able to transport it all.'

'Who is it from?'

'Mr Bergström.'

Flora raised her eyebrows. Mr Bergström was their neighbour at home in the city. He was a real grumpy old sourpuss, but Mum used to help him fill out forms and things because his eyesight wasn't so good. In return, Mr Bergström had promised to water their house plants while they were in Helmersbruk.

'Has Mr Bergström sent us Christmas presents?'

'No, but I asked him to forward our mail here. And I asked him to send something else as well...'

Mum tore the tape off the package and opened it carefully. There was a thick yellow envelope at the top of the box, the type people keep important papers in.

'What's this?'

'Ah, those are the papers I was talking about, things I need to sort out about Dad. But look...'

Mum rummaged around in the box until she found what she was looking for. She looked up at Flora and smiled.

'Well, Flick. I explained to Uncle Bergström that we'd forgotten something important, so he found it and sent it along too.'

Mum lifted a smaller box out of the large box. Flora recognized it immediately.

'Oh, Mum...' Flora began but the words got stuck in her throat.

It was that scuffed old box of Grandma's Christmas baubles! The ones that Dad and Flora would always hang on the tree so lovingly every Christmas Eve.

They were really here!

Flora carefully took the box. It almost felt warm, as if it contained Christmas itself.

The lump in Flora's throat grew even larger. Dad had inherited these baubles from Grandma. And now Flora was inheriting them from Dad.

Dad...

Mum glanced at the large man's wristwatch that Flora was still wearing on her wrist.

'Well, you know, Flick... it was silly of me not to bring our Christmas decorations. We have to stick to as many traditions as we can, even if Christmas will be different this year.'

'But we don't have a Christmas tree.'

'Oh yes we do. I bought one at the market. It's outside, at the bottom of the steps.'

Flora ran to the door and looked out. It was only a tiny fir, but the branches looked sturdy. Dad would have deemed it worthy of Grandma's prized possessions.

'It's perfect.'

Mum looked happy.

'Have you spoken to Fridolf?'

'About what?'

'About Christmas Eve! Ann-Britt said she can come.'

Flora hadn't really felt like inviting him, and she still didn't.

She couldn't help being angry at him for just giving up and letting Dagmar Marton build her hotel. The manor was his, of course, so it was up to him, but still...

'Well?' said Mum. 'Have you?'

'No. But I will,' said Flora.

She opened the box and looked inside. The antique baubles were beautiful, with patterns in yellow, red and violet. They were all intact. She put the lid back on and caressed it lovingly.

Flora had never really looked at the box itself. She had always been too impatient to lift the lid and admire the baubles.

But now as she sat there and inspected the slightly dented old cardboard box, she saw that there was something written in ink, in old-fashioned handwriting, on the lid.

The text was difficult to decipher.

With hi... heartfelt wishes for a... joyful Christmas to our dear...

Our dear who? That exact spot had got wet at some point and the ink was smudged.

Mum unpacked a bag of food that she had also dragged home on the sledge.

'It's not going to be a fancy Christmas dinner, just some herring and potatoes for starters. We can make the meatballs tonight, and I bought some ready-made carrot mash, because nobody really likes swede mash, and then gingerbread and mulled wine for afters. Ann-Britt offered to bring dessert. Sound good?'

'Mm.'

Flora leant closer to the lid of the box and followed the text with her finger, as if that would make it clearer. Had Grandma's prized possessions always been in this box? They must have, because each bauble had its own little pocket of tissue paper.

Ki... os. Is that what it said?

'Did you ever meet Dad's mother?' Flora asked.

'No, sadly. She died right about the same time as your father and I got together. If we'd been a bit quicker about it, I would have been able to meet her.'

'What a pity.'

Flora suddenly remembered that she had promised the lawyer Agaton Brecht that she would ask Mum something.

'Oh, Mum? How did we end up coming here? To Helmersbruk. Like, did you respond to an advert somewhere, or how did it happen?'

Mum poked her head out from behind the refrigerator door with a surprised look on her face.

'Uh... let me think. I asked everyone I knew if they had any tips for somewhere we could go for a bit of a break. But who the heck was it that suggested this particular place?'

She slammed the refrigerator door and looked pensive.

'Could it have been someone at the publishing house? No, probably not...'

Flora continued trying to read the box.

Maybe the first letter wasn't a K at all but an R?

Ri...os. Or maybe *Ri...or.*

'Ah yes, I remember now!' said Mum.

Flora looked up.

'Well?'

'I'm actually not sure who told me about this place,' said Mum. 'That's what was so strange.'

'What do you mean?'

'A postcard came through the letter box. It was an old black-and-white photograph of the Gatekeeper's Cottage. On the back it said "This house is at your disposal" with the address underneath. So I wrote and said we'd like to rent the house, and a week or so later Fridolf replied and said that we were welcome. Actually no, he phrased it more strangely. "Mrs Winter is welcome to try," he wrote. Whatever that was supposed to mean.'

Flora understood exactly what Fridolf had meant.

They were welcome as far as Fridolf was concerned, but ultimately it was up to the manor. Still, there was something else she didn't understand.

'So who sent that postcard?' said Flora.

'I wondered that too,' said Mum. 'It didn't have our address on it, so it hadn't arrived in the mail. I'd asked so many people for suggestions, I just assumed one of them was passing by and posted it through one day when we were out. I'm sure that's what must have happened.'

Mum looked satisfied that the mystery had been explained.

Flora had a different theory.

A manor that could open and close doors, leave clues and select who was allowed to enter its grounds.

A manor with a will of its own.

Couldn't a manor like that get a postcard sent to someone it wanted to summon?

'You wanted us to come here. And we came,' Flora whispered, feeling the hairs on the back of her neck stand on end.

'Did you say something?' said Mum.

She had opened all the yellow envelopes and was sorting papers on the kitchen table. She let out a sad sigh.

'Oh, Rupert, Rupert,' she murmured.

Flora stood up and gave her a hug.

All these papers with Dad's name on them—it seemed so pitiful. Like all that was left of him was a wristwatch, a box of Christmas baubles and a bunch of documents with tiny text.

'What is it you have to do?' Flora asked, still hugging her mother.

'I just have to fill in some forms and make sure I have all the necessary papers so that everything goes smoothly with the inheritance and that sort of thing.'

'Inheritance?'

'Yes. Dad didn't own much and you're his only child, so it should be easy to figure out. But our lawyer said that Dad never really sorted out his mother's affairs when she died, and that makes things a little tricky.'

'Why didn't he?'

Mum laughed, but Flora saw tears glistening in her eyes.

'You know what your father was like. Not very practical about these sorts of things. He probably figured he'd get round to it later and just put all the papers in a pile somewhere. And then... well, then he got sick.'

That very pile must have been what Mum was going through right now on the kitchen table. A lot of big brown envelopes with stamps and scribbles on them. It would probably take a long time for her to read through everything.

'Can I help you?' asked Flora.

'Yes, please, if you don't mind. Could you open any envelopes not already opened and check the dates on the documents inside? We can start by putting everything in chronological order.'

'OK.'

Flora reached for one of the envelopes and tore it open with her finger. The paper had become so thin and brittle that it almost felt like soft cloth.

She pulled out a wedge of papers with a handwritten note on top.

Dear Mr Winter,

Please find enclosed the documents that your mother kept with us. She stipulated that they be sent to you in the event of her death.

With deepest sympathy.

Sincerely,

Rakel Hansen

Fauré & Simonson Legal

'I think these must be Grandma's papers,' said Flora.

'Oh good! Put them in the right order then, please, and don't lose anything.'

'I won't.'

Flora began to work her way through the pile, but it was slow going. There were a lot of confusing words and illegible handwritten comments.

Attestation, certification, power of attorney, testament. Did Mum understand this sort of thing?

In the pile she also found a small envelope that didn't look quite as dreary as the rest. It appeared to be a letter. The envelope was still sealed.

To Rupert. To be opened after my death.

Rupert, that was Dad. But who was the letter from? It must be from his mother!

A letter that Dad had never got a chance to read. It was so sad. What if Grandma had written something really loving to Dad?

Flora took out a butter knife and was just about to open the envelope when she heard a voice coming from the hallway.

'Yoo-hoo?'

It was Ann-Britt.

Mum got up at once and ran her hands through her hair as if to tidy it.

'Hello there!'

'I hope I'm not disturbing your Christmas preparations?'

'I wish. We're struggling through probate.'

'Probate? The night before Christmas Eve?'

Mum sighed and looked at all the papers on the kitchen table.

'Yeah, you're right. I finally finished my book yesterday, so I thought it was time to tackle this. But maybe we should focus on drumming up a bit of Christmas spirit instead and deal with this afterwards...'

'In that case, I have just the thing!' said Ann-Britt. 'There's a Christmas concert in the church in half an hour. You should come!'

'Well...' said Mum, looking hesitantly at Flora. 'Flora's been sick, so I don't know.'

'You go without me,' said Flora. 'I'll be fine. We'll have plenty of time to make meatballs tomorrow.'

'Are you sure?'

'Absolutely.'

'OK, well, in that case, I'd love to,' Mum said to Ann-Britt. 'Just give me a minute to change.'

She disappeared up into her bedroom. Ann-Britt winked at Flora.

'Seems the spell must be broken. I just walked straight through the gate this time.'

Flora nodded sadly. Now that Fridolf had unlocked the main gate, anyone could enter the manor grounds, be they friend or foe.

'What have you got there?' Ann-Britt said, pointing to the box of Christmas baubles.

Flora lifted the lid. Ann-Britt whistled, impressed.

'They're spectacular. You don't see a lot of those these days. They were only produced for a short time here at the glass factory, and they were probably too expensive for most people.'

'Huh?' Flora exclaimed. 'They made Christmas baubles here? In Helmersbruk?'

'Yes. Take good care of them, they're bound to be worth a tidy sum. Did you find them here in the Gatekeeper's Cottage?'

'No...'

Flora carefully put the lid back on. Mum came down the stairs. She had put on her best pink sweater and some lipstick. She looked very pretty.

'Flick, remember to talk to Fridolf about tomorrow.'

'I will. Have fun,' said Flora.

Mum and Ann-Britt disappeared into the winter evening. The kitchen was silent.

Flora picked up the letter and butter knife again and carefully opened the envelope.

A few photographs fell on the kitchen floor as she took out a stack of handwritten papers.

Flora read the one on top.

My dearest, apple of my eye. At the time of writing, I am in Helmersbruk, having returned for the last time. The doctors say I don't have much time left now.

The letter slipped out of Flora's fingers and fell on to the rag rug.

It couldn't be.

Helmersbruk. The letter to Dad mentioned Helmersbruk!

Dad had never mentioned the place.

Flora bent down and picked up one of the fallen photographs. It was a black-and-white portrait of a smiling young woman wearing a hat. A flat velvet hat with a narrow brim. Even though it was grey in the picture, Flora knew what colour the hat really was.

Red.

Flora was stunned. Everything was starting to fall into place.

She picked the letters up from the rug, sat down on the kitchen floor and began to read.

FORTUNE AND TRAGEDY

Well, my darling.

I am on the train now, hence the shaky handwriting. Helmersbruk is behind me and I don't think I will ever return. I did manage to visit Papa's grave. I brought a bunch of red roses to lay on the von Hiems family grave too, but I couldn't bring myself to go near it.

In any case, we shall soon be reunited, Robert and I.

Back to my story. We got up to the final autumn. Autumn 1925.

Papa was working on the labyrinth from morning to night. He said he had to plant all the bushes before the ground froze or it wouldn't be ready in time for the wedding the following summer.

He would often go out before I woke up in the mornings, and go to bed straight after supper because he was so exhausted.

Then came the terrible evening when he didn't come in for dinner. I knew at once that something was wrong, so I ran out into the gardens to look for him.

Just then, the first snowflakes of winter started falling from a grey sky. Papa didn't answer when I called, but I could guess where he was.

He was lying on the grass in his labyrinth, still gripping the handle of his shovel. His eyes were open and his gaze was directed towards the sky.

I knelt down beside him and carefully closed his eyes so he wouldn't get snow in them.

For a while I just sat there holding his cold, calloused hand in mine. I don't know why I didn't cry. The tears just didn't come.

Then I dragged myself into the manor's kitchen and announced:

'My father is dead. He is lying in the labyrinth. Can someone help me carry him out?'

Mr Gustafsson the gatekeeper and Gonny came to the rescue, while Asta the cook called the doctor, though it was too late for that.

We laid Papa out in his bed. I unlaced his muddy boots and washed his hands with warm water and a kitchen towel. I still didn't cry. In fact, I was very composed and practical, and when there was a knock on the door and the factory director himself stepped in, closely followed by a teary-eyed Gonny, I nodded at them and said:

'No need to worry, he had very almost finished the labyrinth.'

'Dear Rigmor,' said the director. 'Please don't worry about that.'

But I remained stubborn.

'It was important to him that the labyrinth be ready for the wedding. I can finish it myself.'

The director nodded.

'I am very sorry for your loss, Rigmor,' he said after a while.

'Thank you, sir,' I said with a bob.

He left our little house with Gonny in tow. But just before he left, Gonny turned to me and whispered:

'I've sent a message to Robert.'

Papa was buried in the Helmersbruk cemetery a week after his death. Trust a gardener to pass away just before the first frost. If he had died just a few weeks later, we would have had to wait until the spring before we could dig a grave.

Robert didn't show up. He probably didn't have time. It would have taken too long to get to Helmersbruk from the glassworks in Central Europe.

It was a simple funeral with only a handful of mourners.

Mr Gustafsson, his wife, Margit, Asta, Gonny, the priest and me.

As soon as the grave was filled, I planted forty flower bulbs in the soil. Grape hyacinths, tulips, dahlias and daffodils. I wanted the head gardener's grave to be in full bloom the following spring. It would brighten up the entire cemetery, which at the time was dark and colourless.

But where would I be when the daffodils poked out of the ground? Not in Helmersbruk, I knew that much.

The orangery wasn't the only place where life was blooming and growing.

I could barely button my coat, and even my cheeks had become rounder. It was lucky that I was heavily built to begin with, so people probably just assumed I had been eating more than usual.

Robert had been gone for months, so he didn't know about it either.

What would the factory director and his wife have said if they knew about the baby growing inside me?

What became of people like me? Unmarried women with no family to support them when they bore their illegitimate child?

As soon as the labyrinth was finished, I would head to another town to look for work. I had some savings and a small inheritance from Papa, so I could get by for a little while.

I wouldn't miss Helmersbruk all that much. But I would miss Gonny and my beloved little Freddy. And Robert, of course. I could hardly bear to think about him.

But there was no other solution.

I went through Papa's things. I would give the books to Mr Gustafsson. Perhaps the church would take his clothing and donate it to the less fortunate. The furniture wasn't ours, so it would have to stay, and I thought I might as well leave Papa's tools in the orangery for the next gardener.

His old music box, the one that played a Christmas tune when it was wound, would make an excellent christening gift. Papa would have liked his grandson to have his music box.

Then there were my own possessions. They were even fewer. I would only take my clothes, a few photographs, my red velvet hat in its box, and the beautiful Christmas baubles that the lady of the house had gifted me. One day I would have my own home with a sturdy little Christmas tree, I decided.

One evening, when I had almost finished packing, there was a knock on the door of the head gardener's residence.

I thought it might be Asta bringing me some supper, as she had been doing all week because I had been too weary to make it up to the main house.

But it wasn't Asta. It was Robert.

I had never dreamt of a big wedding with a veil, train and flowers everywhere. Our wedding was more beautiful than anything I could have hoped for.

I wore my best dress, which only just about fit me. Robert wore one of his simpler suits. The officiant glanced at my belly. He probably knew what was going on but thought it was good that we were getting married anyway, even if it was a few months late.

We had taken the automobile to another town. Robert thought that would be best. He had broken off his engagement to Wilhelmina Marton earlier the same day. She was upset and furious, which I could understand. I might have felt sorry for her if I hadn't been on cloud nine myself.

Because it had happened, against all odds.

Robert von Hiems was my husband.

We would go away, he said, travel south to somewhere in Europe and find a nice place where we could settle down and wait for our little baby to come.

Robert didn't want a manor or a glass factory.

Gonny would have to take over the factory instead, he said. He would do a great job.

We promised before God Almighty that we would love each other till death do us part.

We had no idea how soon that would be.

I stayed at a hotel in the town where we got married while Robert went to Helmersbruk to inform his family of the marriage. They would no doubt be upset, he said, so he didn't want me to have to deal with it.

It saddened me that I wouldn't get a chance to say goodbye to Gonny and Freddy, so I gave Robert careful instructions.

I wrote a little letter to Freddy for Robert to leave in his bed along with my beloved teddy bear Morris.

I also wrote a long letter to Gonny. I hoped he would understand

and forgive us. After all, he was the one whose future would be most affected by our marriage.

I gave Robert a list of the things I had left behind in our haste to elope. The music box, the shoebox full of his letters and the red velvet hat were still in the house that used to be Papa's and my home. Robert promised to collect them.

And then we would make a fresh start. A new country and a new life with our own little family.

Robert was taking his time, I thought. I expected him to come back that evening, but he didn't. I wasn't worried; I supposed he had decided to spend the night at the manor and drive back in daylight.

It was our wedding night and Christmas Eve, so I felt a little lonely in the hotel. But then I felt a tiny, tiny movement inside my belly and was reminded that I wasn't alone. I would never be alone again.

I had a husband now, and soon I would have a child as well. I had a feeling that you were a boy. Your name would be Klaus Rupert. Klaus after Papa. Rupert was Robert's suggestion.

Eventually I fell asleep in the big hotel bed, convinced that Robert would wake me with a kiss, like Sleeping Beauty.

The next day I woke up in a daze and made my way down to the breakfast room. I heard some of the other guests talking about a terrible accident in the next town over.

Then there were the newspaper headlines in thick black letters.

CHRISTMAS TRAGEDY IN HELMERSBRUK–
FACTORY DIRECTOR, WIFE AND SONS
KILLED IN AUTOMOBILE ACCIDENT!

I don't know what happened when Robert went home to tell his family he had married the gardener's daughter.

I know they must have been hurt and angry, but how did they all end up in the car that veered off the factory bridge and ended up in the rapids?

The director detested that automobile and preferred to travel by horse-drawn carriage. What was different on this occasion?

And now the entire von Hiems family was gone.

I didn't return to Helmersbruk for the funerals. It was too painful.

I didn't contact anyone. As Robert von Hiems's widow, I must have been entitled to some sort of inheritance, but I didn't want anything.

I was consumed with grief and guilt. It was because of me that Robert went home that Christmas Eve when the roads were as slippery as glass. He never would have died if it hadn't been for me. None of them would have died. The director, Madam, Robert, Egon and Fridolf.

It was my fault.

I didn't want Robert's surname after that. I felt like I had stolen it.

The only thing that kept me going was the baby I was carrying.

You were my saviour.

Klaus Rupert Winter, you were born in the capital city a few months later. You were a sweet, quiet baby, much like your uncle Freddy. I chose the name Winter for us because I liked the sound of the word.

I got a job in a florist's and you spent your days with our neighbour Elsie.

We made a cosy little home for ourselves. I hope I gave you a good, safe and loving start in life, like the one my father, your grandfather Klaus, gave me.

At the time of writing, the doctor has given me only a few months to live. My once strong body is now bony and fragile.

No one would call me robust nowadays.

Thank goodness you're an adult now. You keep gushing about a young woman you have met. A beautiful, intelligent woman who is following her dream of working as a writer.

One fine day you will probably have a baby of your own. I think they will be a delightful little person who inherits their mother's literary talent and father's analytical mind and warm heart. Maybe even their grandma's green fingers too? I probably don't have that many other talents to contribute.

Dear Rupert, it was never my intention to mislead you about your family. What I have told you has all been true.

I told you that your father Robert was the best, kindest, most handsome man who ever lived.

I told you that your father's whole family died in an accident.

I told you that your uncles would have loved you dearly, as would your grandfather Klaus.

I haven't been able to tell you about the manor, the estate and the factory. Probably because I am still too stricken with guilt.

But I know that you are not greedy, not someone who craves wealth and possessions. So I hope that you won't be angry with your old mother when you eventually read this letter and find out who your relatives were.

Dear Rupert, forgive me if I made a mistake in not telling you the whole truth. It was, of course, thanks to you that I lived a happy life after all the tragedy.

I have come to terms with the fact that I will have to leave this world without ever knowing what really happened at the von Hiems manor in Helmersbruk on the 24th of December 1925. Perhaps you will solve the mystery one day when I am gone.

But I am looking forward to seeing my Robert again.

Until we meet again,
Mama—Rigmor Winter
20th December 1961

THE TURRET

Flora read the letter three times from start to finish. After the third reading, she cried for a long time. She couldn't help it.

Rigmor's letter to her son Rupert.

Grandma's letter to Dad.

Grandma, who grew up right here, on the von Hiems estate in Helmersbruk.

And Flora's grandfather was Robert von Hiems. The eldest son of the last factory director.

Which meant that Flora was... no, it was too much to get her head around!

Flora felt small and powerless. She wasn't smart enough, old enough, important enough for any of this. She had fantasized about having some sort of connection to the manor, but this was just too much. What was she going to do now?

After sobbing in a heap on the kitchen floor for a while, she managed to get to her feet.

On the kitchen table was the box of Grandma's baubles. And

now Flora could clearly see what was written on the lid. It seemed strange that she didn't see it right away.

With heartfelt wishes for a joyful Christmas to our dear Rigmor, J v H.

J v H must be Jacobina von Hiems. The wife of the last factory director. The woman who hired Rigmor the gardener's daughter as a nanny and gave her some beautiful Christmas baubles as a gift.

With trembling hands, Flora folded the letter and put it back in the envelope. Rigmor was none other than Flora's own grandmother. Dad had only ever spoken about 'my mother' or 'your grandmother' and never mentioned her name. And Flora had never thought to ask.

Now she knew.

If only Grandma Rigmor had plucked up the courage to cross the bridge that last time she visited Helmersbruk just before her death.

Then she might have found her little Freddy alive and well in the Washhouse. He hadn't died in the accident as Rigmor had thought. And Fridolf believed that 'Ringo' had abandoned him. Her letter and the gift of Morris the teddy bear had showed up fifty years too late.

It was all so heartbreakingly sad.

What am I supposed to do now? Flora thought desperately. *Who should I talk to? Does this change anything? Is it too late to save the manor? Should I just keep quiet?...*

Then she realized exactly who she needed to talk to.

Egon. She had to find Egon. Or Gonny, as Grandma had called him.

Flora had so many questions and Egon had the answers. He wouldn't be allowed to sneak away this time. She wouldn't take her eyes off him.

But how would Flora find him? He wasn't exactly at her beck and call.

Although maybe she had been looking in all the wrong places. She had searched the grounds of the estate for a little house where Egon lived with his family. Now she realized that he used to live in the manor house itself. Maybe he was still there.

Then it dawned on her.

Egon loved his library, which was in the turret. Rigmor had even mentioned it in her letter.

Could he be up there now?

Flora went to her room, took the red velvet hat out of its box and put it on. She adjusted Dad's wristwatch, which was still showing 6.30 p.m. on the 24th of December.

She wanted Dad and Grandma to be with her. The watch and hat made them feel a little closer.

Down in the living room, she collected all the porcelain figurines from the bookshelf and wrapped them up in mittens and woolly socks before stuffing them into her jacket pockets. They were coming with her. She decided they didn't belong in the Gatekeeper's Cottage. They had come from the manor house and that was where they would return.

And off she went.

The park was bathed in moonlight as she walked briskly towards the house. The moon cast long shadows over the snow and it was almost as bright as day. The snow sparkled and stars shone in the indigo sky.

It was a beautiful scene, like a painting, but there was no time to stop and admire the view. In the flower beds, the blooming snow roses were so vital and vibrant that it looked like they were straining to see better.

She pounded firmly on the manor door.

'Let me in. I'm going to the turret.'

The door swung open.

Flora went straight up the stairs, past all the paintings, past the closed double doors and up again to the second floor.

She had expected the corridor to be pitch-black like the last time she had been here, but one of the doors in the corridor was ajar, letting in a faint streak of light.

Flora walked up to the door.

'Oh my...'

She stood on the threshold of the turret room and looked in. It was just as she had imagined it! High bookshelves stretched all the way to the ceiling; she was inside a cylinder of books. A long ladder stretched up to the very top shelves, and there, halfway up the ladder, sat Egon.

He was deeply engrossed in a book. As usual, he was dressed in his green trousers and sweater, with a cap pulled down over his brown hair and his glasses slightly askew.

'Good evening, Egon,' Flora said quietly.

He looked up.

'Well, there she is.'

'Mm.'

He smiled.

'It really is remarkable. Every time I see you, you look more like her.'

'Like Rigmor, you mean?'

'That's right.'

'Did you know she was my grandmother?'

He sat still for a moment, then nodded.

'I see that now.'

'Which would make you my?... Let me see. Great-uncle?'

'Grand uncle?' Egon suggested and Flora couldn't help but laugh. It sounded so formal. But then she pulled herself together. They had serious things to talk about.

'Egon. We need to talk about that night,' she said. 'About Christmas Eve 1925.'

'I don't really feel like it,' said Egon. He sounded irritated, which was unlike him.

'I understand it must be difficult. But, Egon, this is important.'

He sighed deeply, put his book on a shelf and climbed down the ladder.

'Might as well get it over with, I suppose. The truth is: the accident was my fault.'

'What do you mean?'

'I mean that if it hadn't been for me, everyone would have survived.'

Flora looked at him in wonder. Egon wasn't the first to claim that the tragedy was their fault. Rigmor had blamed herself in the letters. Fridolf had also said he was responsible. But they couldn't all be to blame, could they?

'What happened?'

Egon crossed his arms over his chest and hunched over as if to make himself smaller.

'Robert came home on Christmas Eve. We were just about to sit down to supper when he arrived. He said he wasn't going to stay, he only wanted to tell us something.'

'That he and Rigmor had got married and were leaving?'

'Precisely. All hell broke loose, of course. Father was furious and Mother was beside herself. Freddy was frightened and ran away to hide. But Robert was adamant. It was all arranged, he explained, and there was nothing anyone could do to stop him from following his heart.'

'Did you know that Robert and Rigmor were in love?'

'Oh yes... I had known for a long time. But I had never considered what it might mean for me...'

Egon sighed.

'Something snapped in me, Miss Flora. Father asked Robert who he thought was going to take over the glass factory when he went off gallivanting around the continent with his floozy. And Robert replied that "Egon would do it"—Egon would be the next factory director. And then... then I blacked out.'

'What do you mean? You fainted?'

'I had some sort of attack. I used to get them when I was a child but thought I had got past them. The next thing I remember was everybody sitting in Robert's automobile. Father, Mother, Robert and I. He was driving so fast, the car was swerving this way and that...'

'They must have been taking you to the doctor!'

'That is my fear. That everybody jumped into the automobile for my sake. That the accident never would have happened had I not been so frail and pathetic...'

Flora walked a few steps closer to Egon and tried to make eye contact.

'Egon, listen. This was not your fault! It was an accident—no more, no less.'

Egon put his hand in his pocket and took out a very wrinkled scrap of paper.

'She wrote to me,' he said quietly. 'Rigmor wrote and asked for my forgiveness in case Robert's decision compelled me to do something against my wishes. She was the only one who even thought about my feelings. The only one who understood...'

He turned his back on Flora. She realized that he wanted her to leave.

'It wasn't your fault, Egon,' she said once more before leaving the turret room.

She walked slowly through the corridor and back down the stairs. Halfway down, it hit her.

'I suppose I've solved the riddle.'

Surely this is what the von Hiems manor had been trying to tell her?

That Flora wasn't just any old tenant; she was the granddaughter of Robert von Hiems.

That's why they had been summoned there, she and Mum. And that was probably why she felt so at home in Helmersbruk. It was where she belonged. She had Helmersbruk in her blood.

But what now? What was she supposed to do with all this information? Would anyone listen to her?

She was standing in front of the tall double doors that had previously been locked.

This time they were ajar, and a crackling fire inside was spreading its warm glow all the way up the stairs.

Flora opened the door and paused on the threshold.

She needed a moment to take in the sight.

It was as if time in the manor had stood still ever since that fateful Christmas Eve fifty years before. The furniture, curtains, paintings, everything was still there. Even the Christmas decorations.

A huge Christmas tree, which had long since lost its needles but still managed to hold its ornaments, stood by one wall. The candles were still attached to the branches. Their wicks were still white. They hadn't even had a chance to light the Christmas tree candles on that Christmas Eve.

Flora looked around at all the traditional Christmas decorations: Yule goats, elf dolls, paper garlands, and wrapped packages under the tree. In the soft glow from the fireplace, the room was very beautiful, if a little spooky.

Flora heard a creak and realized that someone was sitting in one of the armchairs in front of the fireplace. She stepped forward.

'Good evening, Fridolf.'

He didn't look up.

'Good evening, Flora Winter.'

She slowly sat down in the other armchair.

'Is... is this the first time you've... since that evening... the first time you've been here?'

'Mm.'

'Why did you come here now?'

'Because it's my last chance. Before the house is demolished.'

The fire crackled so loudly that it made Flora jump.

'But, Fridolf, surely it doesn't have to be this way? Can't the manor stay as it is, even if you don't want it any more?'

'No. Who can afford to keep an old house like this? It's just as well that someone starts over with something new.'

'But...' Flora said helplessly. 'What about the treasure? The treasure your father hid is yours now! If you found the treasure, you could save the manor. Just imagine!'

'The treasure is gone. Maybe it never existed in the first place.'

Flora wanted to argue. She wanted to persuade him. But she couldn't think of a single thing to say.

'Besides,' Fridolf said dully, 'that accident was my fault.'

Flora was starting to get a bit annoyed at everyone blaming themselves for the car crash.

'Accidents aren't anybody's fault. That's why they're called accidents.'

'But it was.'

'How? You were just a little kid.'

'I remember it like it was yesterday. My brother Robert came home and told me he was going to take Rigmor away from us. My Rigmor.'

'Yes?'

'And I ran out into the snow. I was furious. That he would just take her far away, without even asking me...'

He looked tired, old and childlike all at the same time. He took a deep breath and continued his story.

'Robert's car was out in the courtyard and I thought he wouldn't get far without that. And then they would have to stay with me.'

'Mm-hmm?'

'So I stuck my folding knife into one of the tyres. I thought it would cut right through, but instead the knife got stuck. Then they all came pouring out of the house. Father and Robert were carrying Egon, who seemed to have fallen ill. And I was too cowardly to stop them. I ran away and hid, and then they drove away, Father, Mother, Robert and Egon. So you see. It was my fault.'

Flora shook her head.

'Rigmor thought it was her fault,' she said. 'And so does Egon. But an accident is an accident. The past can't be changed.'

Fridolf shifted his position in the armchair, which creaked ominously under his weight. He had Morris the teddy bear in his pocket, Flora noticed.

Now he looked at her with sadness in his eyes.

'I waited and waited,' he muttered. 'I sat over there by the tree. But they never came back.'

'I came back,' said Egon, who suddenly appeared on the rug in front of the fire.

'Yes,' said Fridolf. 'You are kind, Gonny. You came back to me.'

The brothers smiled at each other and Flora felt as if she was intruding on something that wasn't really her business. She looked up at the mantelpiece instead. On it she saw a funny little house, like a doll's house. On the roof was a star made of gold-painted wood.

'What's that?' Flora wondered.

'It's the stable,' said Egon. 'Where we used to display our nativity scene.'

Flora began rummaging through her pockets. One by one, she set the porcelain figurines in the stable. The angel from the gatekeeper's pocket. The shepherd from the flower bed. The donkey and the ox from the stable.

'Rigmor thought you were all dead,' she said as she arranged the figurines.

'How come?'

'It said in the newspaper that the director, his wife and sons had died. It didn't say *how many* sons. So she thought you were dead too, Fridolf. Otherwise, I'm sure she would have come looking for you...'

Fridolf said nothing and Flora continued arranging the nativity scene.

The first wise man from Ann-Britt's shoe. The second from the library. The third from under Agaton Brecht's hat.

She sat back down in the armchair.

'Now they're all there. Except the family.'

'Mm,' mumbled Fridolf. 'The family, that's what's missing.'

And they sat in silence.

THE DIRECTORS

When Flora woke up, she didn't understand where she was at first. It was cold and dark, her nose felt tickly, and her body ached.

With effort, she sat up and realized she was in the great hall of the von Hiems manor. She must have fallen asleep.

The fire had burnt out. Fridolf was still in the armchair with Morris in his arms, snoring quietly. Egon was nowhere to be seen.

It must have been late. Flora looked at her father's wristwatch, even though it was still showing the wrong time.

'Fridolf? We should probably go now... Mum will be wondering where I've got to.'

But Fridolf didn't wake up. Flora couldn't help him back to the Washhouse on her own, but she couldn't very well just leave him there either.

She walked towards the double doors and tried to push them open.

But she couldn't—the doors were locked!

'Let me out!' Flora said insistently.

The doors stood firm.

'Hello?' said Flora even louder. 'I have to leave now! I'll come back later. Open up!'

She heard a scratching sound at the other end of the room and saw something white scuttling across the floor. The squirrel! How had it got in?

Flora watched the squirrel until it disappeared under the bare Christmas tree. Just then, incredible things started to happen.

Flames came alive on all the candles on the needleless tree! A fire roared to life in the fireplace again. The crystal chandelier on the ceiling, which was so covered in cobwebs that it looked like it was draped in chiffon fabric, lit up too.

It was as if the whole room had woken from its slumber. Everything woke up, except Fridolf, who continued to sleep.

And in front of Flora, in the middle of the floor, was a package.

Hesitantly, she moved closer.

To Flora, it said on the label. Unlike everything else in the room, the package didn't look in the least bit dusty. It was wrapped in the old-fashioned way, in brown paper with red sealing wax.

'For me?' whispered Flora.

Did she dare open it? It wasn't Christmas yet.

Though it couldn't be long before midnight, so it was almost Christmas Eve, at least...

She carefully tore open the paper. Inside the package was a beautiful little wooden box.

Flora took a deep breath and opened it.

Inside was a tiny Christmas tree that started to spin. A melody played, one that Flora had heard many times. She sang along. She knew all the words.

'O Tannenbaum, o Tannenbaum wie treu sind deine Blätter...'

Fridolf grunted contentedly in his armchair but still didn't wake up.

There was something else in the box as well, at the very bottom.

Flora picked up the object and smiled when she saw what it was.

As the music box continued to play its melody, over and over again, Flora walked over to the nativity scene and placed the porcelain Jesus right in the middle.

A little baby with a halo.

But where were his parents? Mary and Joseph were still on their way. They would have to hurry to arrive in time for Christmas.

When Flora turned around again, she almost screamed outright in terror!

Flora and Fridolf weren't alone.

The room was full of people!

Egon was standing behind Fridolf's chair. He looked worried. Flora didn't recognize the others. They were all old men wearing old-fashioned clothes and very serious expressions.

'What is the meaning of this?' said an old man in a white wig.

Flora recognized him. She had seen him in a painting. It was none other than Helmer von Hiems. The very first factory director of Helmersbruk.

'The girl is trying to swindle us, you mark my words,' said another old man.

'But she has von Hiems blood in her veins.'

'A girl as director? Absolutely not.'

'Why ever not?' Egon snapped. 'I doubt there is anything that Flora can't do. You have all managed as directors; I think Flora would do at least as good a job.'

'Quiet, boy. It's out of the question.'

'Isn't anyone going to ask me if I actually want to be a factory director?' said Flora. 'Because I don't. All I want to do is save your manor. Our manor, I mean. Before the Martons demolish it.'

When she mentioned the name Marton, the whole room filled with exasperated haws and grunts.

After the directors had finished their grumbling, Flora heard something else.

'Flora? Floooraaaa! Answer me! Where are you?'

It was Mum's voice coming from outside. And now it sounded like there were several people outside all calling for Flora.

The directors began to mutter again, more anxiously this time.

'Be quiet,' Flora hissed.

'She can't very well be inside,' someone shouted from outside. 'It's locked!'

'Yes, but look, there's a light on in the window up there.'

'Oh my goodness!'

'The door won't budge. Can we break it down?'

The second voice sounded like Ann-Britt. The directors exchanged grim glances. Fridolf smacked his lips peacefully in his sleep.

Then another voice was heard outside. A higher, younger voice.

'I bet she's in there. She might have learnt about a way in from the book we found in the library.'

It sounded like Petra Marton.

The directors went berserk.

'Marton! A Marton invading our property! How dare she? How did she get in?'

'Let them in,' said Flora, 'or at least let me out. They're worried, can't you hear?'

She was speaking directly to the manor. There didn't seem to be much point in trying to reason with the directors.

'Let them in,' she said, 'and you...' She looked sternly at the directors '...you leave Petra alone! It's not her fault she's a Marton. Just calm down.'

Amazingly, both the manor and the directors obeyed. There was a crashing sound on the ground floor as the front door was thrown open, and rapid footsteps and shouts were heard on the stairs. The directors backed into the shadows. Even Egon disappeared, though Flora would have liked him to stay.

The doors to the great hall swung open as well and Mum was the first to come rushing in.

'Thank God,' she shouted when she saw Flora. 'Oh, thank heavens!'

She threw her arms around Flora and hugged her so tight that she almost crushed her ribs.

'Never do that again!' Mum shouted.

Flora was ashamed. She hadn't meant to fall asleep and let Mum come home from the concert to an empty house. She had just been so tired.

After Mum came Ann-Britt. Then Petra Marton and her mother Dagmar. And last but not least, lawyer Agaton Brecht stepped into the room. So many people. Had they all been looking for Flora?

The newcomers stared with wide eyes at the Christmas tree, the fire, the nativity scene and the music box that was still playing merrily despite not having been wound up in a long time. Flora couldn't see the directors any more, but she could hear them murmuring in the corners.

'What on earth?' Ann-Britt exclaimed. 'Has this room been all done up for Christmas ever since 1925?'

Fridolf finally opened his eyes and looked around groggily. 'What's going on?' he said.

'Good evening, Fridolf,' said Agaton Brecht. 'Mrs Marton and I have been looking for you. And Mrs Winter here has been looking for her daughter. How extraordinary that we've found you both at the same time. And in such charming environs!'

'Why have you been you looking for me?' said Fridolf. 'Am I not free to do as I please?'

'I should remind you, Mr von Hiems, that you promised to sign the agreement before the Christmas holidays,' said Dagmar Marton. 'We have all the paperwork right here and I have signed it already.'

'Well,' said Fridolf. 'You'll have to take it up with the heiress to the manor.'

'Excuse me?' said Dagmar Marton. 'And just who might that be?'

'There she is,' said Fridolf, pointing at Flora with his cane.

He seemed genuinely cheerful for once.

Everyone turned to Flora and she felt her cheeks get hot.

Oblivious to their reactions, Fridolf continued: 'The girl is the very image of her grandmother. I was quite taken aback when first I saw her, so I was. Then it took some time before the penny dropped, so to speak.'

Flora was very embarrassed, but Fridolf's friendly gaze made her feel warm inside.

'This here girl is my brother's granddaughter. The last of the von Hiems family. Well, except for yours truly, that is.'

The room became completely silent. Even the directors were quiet. Flora gulped. Everyone was still staring at her. It was very unpleasant.

'Yeah,' she began nervously. 'It's true. My grandmother's name was Rigmor Winter; her father was a gardener here in the old days. And my grandfather was Robert von Hiems, Fridolf's older brother...'

'This can't be!' exclaimed Dagmar Marton. 'What kind of ludicrous notion is this?'

But Agaton Brecht looked interested.

'Is there any documentation to support this?' he said.

'I think so,' said Flora. 'We've got letters from my grandmother. She wrote everything down so my father would know about his past, but he died before ever reading the letters. And then we have a lot of papers. Certificates and stuff.'

Mum had been standing with her mouth wide open for the past few minutes. Now she suddenly came back to life.

'But, Flora, you can't just invent stories like this! I know you're very fond of this old house and want to stay, but you've gone too far. Much too far!'

Another person appeared in the doorway. A tall, slender figure in a hooded duffel coat.

'I'm pretty sure the girl is telling the truth.'

Dagmar Marton gasped.

'Mummy? What are you doing here? Can't you let me handle this by myself?'

Wilhelmina Marton took off her hood and looked around the room with a strange little smile on her face.

'What a beautiful room, still after all these years. I once believed that this would be my home, but fate had other plans...'

The directors started grumbling once more from their shadowy corners, but if Wilhelmina Marton could hear them, she didn't pay them any mind.

'I was engaged to Robert von Hiems, but we were never in love,' she continued calmly. 'He only had eyes for the gardener's daughter. I was prepared to let him go, but our families insisted. It was deeply humiliating. A very good evening to you, Freddy, sitting all the way over there.'

'Hullo,' Fridolf said from his armchair.

Wilhelmina Marton turned to Flora again.

'Of course I was hurt when Robert broke off the engagement. He came to meet me in the stables when I came riding here. He told me how things were. That he loved another. I threw the engagement ring at him in anger, but I was also relieved.'

'But, Mummy, why have you never told me this?' cried Dagmar Marton, tearing off the sunglasses she had been wearing even though it was night.

Everyone was startled by her exclamation. They never would have expected such a show of emotion from this seemingly cold woman. Behind the sunglasses she revealed a pair of bright green eyes filled with tears.

'My whole life I have been told how unfairly the von Hiems family treated us, and that this land is rightfully ours. Then when I finally get close to reclaiming it, you come out with this!'

Wilhelmina Marton ignored her daughter and looked instead at Fridolf.

'It is incredible how much the girl looks like both her grandparents, isn't it, Freddy? You must remember what they looked like, even though you were just a little boy back then.'

Fridolf nodded. Flora noticed that he was clinging tightly to Morris.

'Now listen,' said Flora. 'Is it really necessary to tear down the manor house to build a hotel? The grounds are huge! Wouldn't it be better to build a hotel further down by the sea? You know, closer to the restaurant. There must be a fair way of sharing the land. What do you think, Fridolf?'

Angry mutters erupted in the shadows. The directors clearly didn't like this suggestion one bit.

Dagmar Marton looked stunned.

'You mean you would hand over part of the land to build a hotel?'

'Is that what you're suggesting?' said Fridolf to Flora.

'Yes,' she replied.

Now the directors screamed right out.

Flora saw that Agaton Brecht's lips were moving but couldn't hear what he was saying through the hullabaloo of the directors.

'She has no right! She has no authority! She is only a child, away with her, stop her!'

'Sorry, could you repeat that?' said Flora to Agaton.

'Well, I just wanted to urge you to think carefully. This is an exceptional building, we can all agree on that. But it is dilapidated. Can you really afford to maintain it?'

He turned to Mum. She looked horrified.

'Huh? Me? No, I absolutely cannot afford to maintain a manor! And neither can Flora.'

'But,' Petra chimed in, 'didn't the family who used to live here leave any money behind?'

A contented murmur came from the shadows.

'People have been speculating over this for fifty years,' said Ann-Britt. 'What happened to the von Hiems treasure? Because you don't know either, do you, Fridolf?'

Fridolf shook his head adamantly.

'Wealth and riches have never been my strong point. If anyone finds the treasure, it belongs to Flora.'

The directors started shouting again in the shadows. It was hard to tell whether they were pleased or upset. Maybe they couldn't agree.

Agaton Brecht, Dagmar Marton, Ann-Britt and Mum all started talking over each other. The hum of voices in the room was deafening to Flora, who could hear both the living and the dead at the same time.

Then something landed on Flora's shoulder, something rather heavy and furry. Just then, Flora shouted loudly to drown them all out.

'Quiet!'

Everyone in the room fell silent at once.

The snow-white squirrel had settled down on Flora's shoulder.

'I think I might know where the treasure is,' said Flora.

THE CENTRE OF THE LABYRINTH

The squirrel ran ahead of them over the snow. Flora and Petra followed close behind, then Mum, Ann-Britt and Dagmar Marton, and lastly Wilhelmina Marton and Agaton Brecht helping Fridolf.

They gathered outside the entrance to the labyrinth. The squirrel scampered off to a tree some distance away. Flora couldn't see it but she could feel it watching her from somewhere up there. The directors had gone quiet. They hadn't said a word since the squirrel had come to sit on Flora's shoulder.

'I have to go in alone,' said Flora.

'Over my dead body!' exclaimed Mum.

'I have to. I don't think I'll be able to find it if anyone comes with me. I have to concentrate.'

'What do you mean? Have you been in the labyrinth before?'

'No.'

Mum protested again but Ann-Britt agreed with Flora.

'I think we should trust Flora. And we're right outside if she needs us.'

'No one has ever found their way to the middle,' said Wilhelmina Marton. 'Not even me, and it was supposed to be my wedding present.'

'Can't you just cut down the bushes?' Dagmar Marton suggested.

'Mum, are you out of your mind?' Petra cried out.

But Flora wasn't listening. She took a deep breath and closed her eyes for a moment.

'See you soon,' she said, opened the gate and stepped into the labyrinth.

It was almost like stepping into a soundproof room. She couldn't hear the others' voices. She couldn't hear the wind either, or even the sound of her own feet.

She took a deep breath, all the way down into the pit of her stomach, then exhaled a small cloud of mist that rose up to the starry sky.

'OK. Right... off I go.'

And so Flora began her journey between the green walls. She turned right. Then right again. Then straight past several forks, then left.

But what next?

'Grandma? Grandma Rigmor? Where do I go now?'

All at once, she knew. She had to go right, then straight for quite a long way. It suddenly seemed so obvious which paths to take.

Like how she had just known how to make a fire. And make potato pancakes. And sing in German. And tend to flower beds.

It was as if Rigmor was guiding her. Grandma Rigmor, who had completed the maze after the death of her father the gardener.

The three of them were the only ones who knew the right way to the centre. Klaus, Rigmor and now Flora.

The moon was shining, allowing Flora to clearly see every corner and curve.

It was Christmas Eve. And Flora Winter was making her way through the labyrinth. The last descendant of the von Hiems family.

Right, left, left, straight.

Then all the way down a path that looked like a dead end. But it was an illusion—that was the secret of the labyrinth! The gardener had come up with it and shown his daughter but no one else.

Flora walked down the hidden passage to the centre of the maze.

She rounded the last corner. And there it was.

The centre of the labyrinth was like a room with green walls, with the starry sky as its ceiling and the moon as its light.

There was something in the middle of the space, all covered in snow. Was it a small statue? Or a fountain?

Flora walked up to the object and swept away the snow on top. It appeared to be a small table. How odd. And rather baffling. She had been hoping for a massive treasure chest in the centre of the labyrinth, but instead there was just this strange piece of garden furniture made of stone.

Flora was sure she just needed to think harder. What was she missing?

The snow was light and airy, and the rest of the layer covering the stone slab was easy to sweep away. Now Flora noticed that it wasn't completely smooth. There were carvings in the top and a little spike sticking up in the middle.

The surface almost looked like a clock. Then Flora understood.

It was a sundial. When the sun shone, the shadow of that little spike would show the time.

There was no sunshine now, of course, only moonlight. But the spike still cast a clear shadow across the surface.

What was it pointing to? Flora leant closer to see the carvings in the tabletop.

It was an H. A swirly H.

OK...

Or was the spike pointing to something else? Flora turned around, but all she saw was a dark green wall of bushes, nothing interesting.

Maybe if she crouched so that her eyes were at the same height as the sundial?

She couldn't see anything at first and started grumbling as irately as the directors in the shady corners of the great hall.

The snow on the ground in the centre of the labyrinth was so smooth. It looked like someone had sifted powdered sugar over the grass.

But at the edge, by the roots of the hedge wall, she thought she saw something. Something rectangular!

'A treasure chest!' Flora gasped, lunging forward.

This must be it! It wasn't exactly a chest, but some sort of box. Could she move it? Yes, she could.

Flora dragged the box away from the hedge. It wasn't very heavy, even though it was made of metal.

Her hands were shaking so much she could barely open the clasps.

The lid flew open with a bang and Flora leant forward, excited to see what was inside.

'Oh, give me a break!' she sighed.

Was the manor teasing her? What was the meaning of this?

It wasn't treasure; it was a toolbox. In the box were secateurs, trowels, rakes and various other gardening tools. Nothing valuable that could be sold to save a manor.

Flora had to keep her disappointment at bay for a moment in order to think clearly.

Hang on a minute.

Whose toolbox was it? Were these the tools that Klaus the gardener, Flora's great-grandfather, had used to create the labyrinth? Could it be a clue?

Flora looked down into the box again. Under the tools was something flat. A fat old notebook with a brown leather cover, full of neat handwriting.

When she opened it, something fell out and landed in the snow.

It was Joseph. Joseph from the nativity scene.

Flora felt so warm inside that she didn't even notice her trousers getting soaking wet from the snow.

The porcelain figurine was proof. The notebook was a clue.

But what was it trying to tell her?

Joseph marked a double-page spread in the notebook that looked different from the other pages.

The gardener had kept a journal about his work. Neat and tidy, with bars and columns, calculations, dates and sketches. On this particular page there was a drawing. Flora had to think for a while before she understood what it represented.

It was the orangery. She recognized the spiral staircase, the door and the wall where the garden tools hung.

But what was that? It looked like Klaus had completed the drawing at a later time, with different ink.

Dug at the director's request, 26th July 1924, it read.

Flora wasn't particularly good with drawings and sketches. She held the book up so that the moon would illuminate the page properly.

Unless she was mistaken, it looked as though Klaus had dug a hole inside the orangery. Like an underground cellar, right by the spiral staircase. At the director's request. Why would the director have wanted a pit there?

Could it be...?

Yes, it must be...

Or maybe not.

There was only one way to find out!

She took the notebook with her and followed her own footprints back out of the maze.

The others were waiting outside: Mum, Ann-Britt, Petra, Wilhelmina, Dagmar, Agaton and Fridolf. The squirrel was still nowhere to be seen.

'Did you find the treasure?' Petra asked eagerly.

'Have to check something,' Flora mumbled and started running.

There was no time to explain.

Flora, mistress of the manor, is going to visit her orangery, she thought.

But it wasn't a fantasy any more–it was true! Flora was the mistress of the manor, in a way, and this was her orangery. Hers and Fridolf's.

But above all, the manor really belonged to itself. Perhaps no one could ever really own and make decisions for the von Hiems manor.

Though Flora was more than happy to take care of the manor if it wanted her to, and she got the feeling that it did.

When Flora squeezed through the door, she was struck by an incredible scent.

The whole orangery was in bloom! There were hyacinths and snow roses growing all over the place. The moon shone in through the windowpanes, but in the shadows it was pitch-black.

She heard a rustle as the squirrel slipped in through the door and came to sit on the spiral staircase. It looked curious, as though its little red eyes were sparkling. But it was probably just a reflection of the moonlight.

'Flora?'

It was Mum. The others had caught up with her and were standing outside the orangery, anxiously awaiting a resolution.

'Just give me a minute.'

What did the drawing look like? Where was that hole that the gardener had dug at the director's request?

It had to be there somewhere.

The ground was covered in dry leaves. Flora kicked them away.

Yes, she remembered now. Here were those big stone slabs that Flora had stepped on last time she was here. One of them was bigger than the others. When Flora stepped on it, she found that it rocked slightly.

'I need help lifting something!' Flora called.

Ann-Britt arrived first, quickly followed by the others.

'I think there's something down here,' Flora explained. 'Do you think we can move this stone slab?'

'We can give it a try!' said Ann-Britt.

Flora liked Ann-Britt. No unnecessary questions, no objections. Ann-Britt stepped up straight away.

But it wasn't until Petra Marton and Mum also came to help that they got anywhere.

Ann-Britt found a crowbar in the corner with the other garden tools and used it to lift the stone slab enough for the others to get a hold of it.

'Watch your fingers, girls!' shouted Mum.

'Ready? We'll all lift it off together,' said Ann-Britt.

'Wait!' cried Flora.

She needed to steel herself first.

She had believed she was about to find the treasure so many times and each time she had been disappointed. What if there was nothing under the stone slab at all? What if she was wrong again?

But this felt different. This time, it felt right.

'OK,' she said. 'I'm ready. One–two–three!'

They lifted, pushed and pulled, and together they managed to slide the stone slab over.

Underneath was a pit.

'Move, Mum, you're blocking the moonlight,' Petra said to Dagmar Marton, who immediately did as she was told.

The moon's rays shone down into the pit.

There was a box down there. A large shiny box. It was a rather fancy box too, with a squiggly H on it, just like the H on the main gate down by the Gatekeeper's Cottage. And the H on the sundial in the hedge maze.

Flora realized that everyone was looking at her again.

'Aren't you going to look?' said Petra.

'Yes.'

Flora lay down on her stomach and reached into the hole. The lid of the chest was shut tight and she worried that it might not open.

But the lid gave way and Flora opened the box.

No one spoke for a long time. Everyone was looking down into the pit, at the box and its contents glistening in the moonlight.

Coins with squiggly symbols on them.

Medals and pearls, brooches and necklaces with colourful gemstones.

Spoons and cups made of gold—or perhaps silver? It was hard to see.

And at the top, above the coins and jewellery, was a gently smiling porcelain figure with outstretched arms.

It was the final figure for the nativity scene. Mary. The mother.

Fridolf was the first to say something. He sounded excited.

'Won't somebody help Flora get her treasure out of that hole? Then you're all invited to the Washhouse for some hot soup. I have gingerbread too. Christmas comes but once a year.'

EPILOGUE

CHRISTMAS EVE, 45 YEARS LATER

Long have I existed.

I have seen so much, and so many. They have come and they have gone.

Long I stood, alone and forgotten.

Then she came. And she has never left me.

Sometimes she travels away but she always returns.

Like now! She is approaching.

'Come,' I say.

She replies:

'Yes, yes, I'm coming. Silly old manor.'

How wonderful. She will be here soon.

Helmersbruk is much the same. The church, library and bus stop all look like they used to. The greengrocer's has been torn down and replaced with a supermarket.

'Flora!' someone shouts as she gets off the bus.

Ann-Britt comes walking towards her. No one would think she was over eighty years old; she has barely changed since the day they met at the manor gate all those years ago. Only her hair is whiter.

'You didn't have to come and meet me,' says Flora.

'I know, but it's nice to have a little break from the Christmas bustle. Besides, your mother insisted.'

Flora wants to visit the grave first.

A simple cross stands next to the church wall. Here lies Klaus the gardener, Flora's great-grandfather. The bright snow roses at the foot of the cross are poking out above the snow, as always. Flora lights her first candle and places it among the flowers.

They move on to the von Hiems family grave, where several candles are already glowing in the twilight. It is beautiful. Flora lights her second candle while Ann-Britt brushes some snow off the tombstone.

'Merry Christmas, Fridolf,' Flora murmurs and places the candle directly beneath his name.

'I'm so grateful that he always joined us for dinner in the Gatekeeper's Cottage. Every evening until the day he died!' says Ann-Britt with a sad smile. 'I miss him.'

Flora nods. Dear Fridolf lived to be a hundred years old. No one would have thought it possible, frail as he was when Flora came to Helmersbruk for the first time.

Flora lights a few more candles.

'Merry Christmas, Egon and Grandpa Robert. Say hello to Grandma and Dad for me.'

Then they get into the car and drive away from Helmersbruk town centre, over the new bridge with its sturdy railings. The gleaming facade of Marton Plaza looms a little further ahead.

'Fully booked!' says Ann-Britt. 'Always fully booked. Even over Christmas!'

Flora asks Ann-Britt to drop her off at the end of the avenue instead of driving all the way up to the entrance. She wants to walk through the tunnel of trees and approach the manor house slowly.

She sees the forest lake sparkling between the trees. Flora has had the grounds thoroughly cleared, tidied and planted anew, all according to gardener Klaus's designs. In a few months, everything here will be in full bloom and smell heavenly.

Flora thinks there is nothing more beautiful than the von Hiems manor house in the light of the midwinter moon. Warm light, voices and music spill out from the windows.

Flora takes off her coat and shoes and goes straight up the stairs and into the great hall.

They managed to get a very grand fir tree, several metres high and very sturdy.

The nativity scene is set up on the mantelpiece. The room smells of mulled wine, gingerbread, pine and hyacinths.

Everybody is here. Children, adults, old people. The dead are present too, but they keep to the shadows and seem calm and content.

'Here she comes.'

'Oh good. The director is home.'

The room is teeming with people. Family, friends, neighbours—everybody who wants to celebrate Christmas at the von Hiems manor is welcome. It becomes rather chaotic when all the children want to help decorate the huge tree, but Flora's best friend Petra delegates tasks and makes sure that even the littlest ones have something to hang.

Petra waves and laughs when she sees Flora. They don't have time to chat now, but that doesn't matter. There will be plenty of time later.

Diana comes up to Flora. She is ten years old, Flora's eldest grandchild. She wants to whisper something in her ear.

'Grandma, guess what I saw. A squirrel! A white one! With red eyes. But the others say I'm making it up.'

Flora nods and gives Diana a hug.

'I know you're not making it up. I'll tell you about the squirrel a little later, I promise.'

And then Mum appears. Linn Winter has shrunk a little but her bright eyes don't look old in the slightest.

'You've come just in time, Flick,' she says and hands her a box.

Flora looks at her wristwatch.

Yes, right on the dot. It is Christmas Eve and the time is half-past six.

She clears her voice and makes the announcement everyone has been waiting for.

'Now, children! It's time to hang up Great-grandma Rigmor's most prized possessions. They must be hung from the sturdiest branches. Then we can all celebrate Christmas together!'

ARE YOU READY TO JOIN EVA FRANTZ ON ANOTHER SPOOKY ADVENTURE?

PUSHKIN CHILDREN'S INVITES YOU TO RASPBERRY HILL.

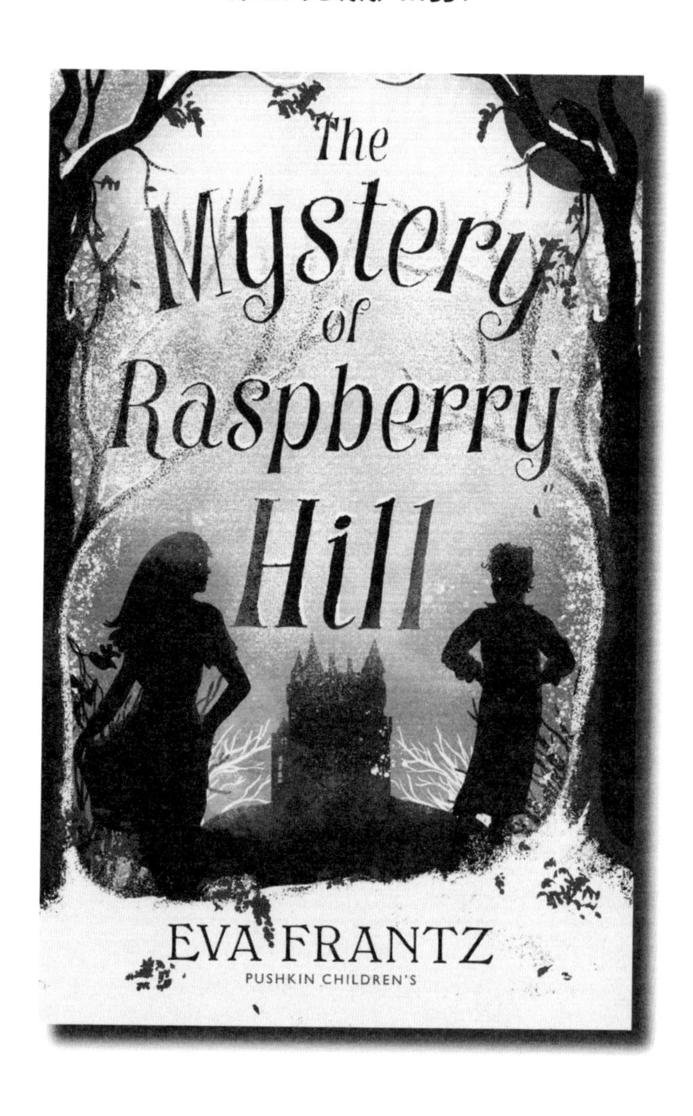